哈福

最新式美語，和美國零時差

流行
美語排行榜

Pop
English Billboard

美國人最愛說的100句話

➡ 最新式美語：說英語，就要與美國同步流行
➡ 駐美英語老師，教您簡單、流行風潮英語，
　快速融入美國生活

 附
MP3

張瑪麗◎著

哈福

最新式美語，
和美國零時差

　　説英語，就要與美國人同步流行！美國人最愛説的流行美語排行榜是那些？你知道了嗎？就讓本書來一一解秘。

　　你是否常覺得，美國現代電影和電視上的英語，並不是你辛辛苦苦在課堂上學到的英語。別再學那些恐龍時代的英語了，因為語言是活的，不管是國語或是英語，都有流行的語言，為年青人廣泛使用著。

　　本書是根據美國現今社會所作的調查，列出最流行的語言。本書中的每一句英語，都是既流行又簡單，每一句都可以現學現説，你只要選你喜歡的流行英語就好了，不需要死背整本書。

本書最大特色是：

　　·**每一個字，你都學過，一定都會**：但連在一起，意思就不一樣了，你一定要知道。例如 Out、of、the、blue，這四個字，你早就都會了，但連在一起，你絕對沒想到，意思竟然 180 度完全不一樣，Out of the blue 是：毫無來由；不知從哪裡冒出來的意思，嚇一跳吧！

　　·**每一句英語都很短，都很簡單**：你知道嗎？Man、Hello、Beats me，一、二個字，就可説很流行的英語了，你一定要學會。

　　·**每一個句型的用法**：都詳細解説真正的意思和用法，

並有舉一反三的類似語、相反語句，和會話靈活運用。

　　·**每一句都是美國人天天說的流行語**：移民、留學、觀光、考察、上班、洽商，Easy 又 Happy，現學可現用。

　　又如打招呼，你可曾聽過兩個人見面說：Hey, what's up?，或是把手舉起來說 Give me five.，如果沒有，那可就太遜了。從這裡可以看出，用最簡單的單字，用你小學或中學，學過的英語，就可以說一口好英語了。

　　《流行美語排行榜：美國人最愛說的 100 句話》精心選出時下最流行的上榜英語，不分年齡大小，時時刻刻都可以派得上用場。例如男女交朋友常用的字：甩了女朋友，被女朋友甩了，兩人吹了，英語都有流行的詞語。美國年輕人已不再說 fall in love with 這種老式英語了。排行榜上的 have a crush on 某人，才能表達 21 世紀的愛。

　　另外，女孩子愛說的「真噁心」，年青人愛用的話「蹺課」、「拍馬屁」，說某個女孩子是「花瓶」，都是流行榜上的英語，這些英語不僅現代感十足，而且都很簡單。

　　表示情緒的話，例如生氣，用 angry 已落伍了，說 pissed off 才夠酷。還有抓狂、閃遠一點、神氣什麼，最酷的說法是什麼呢？書中均有詳盡的解說。

　　流行語拉近你與世界的距離，如果能夠活學活用，你就算是與美國人同步流行了，跟得上英語的流行的腳步了，本書讓你走在世界流行的尖端！

CONTENTS

Chapter 7

Chapter 8

Chapter 10

Chapter 1

What's up?

有什麼鮮事嗎？

Hey, John. What's up?

嗨，約翰，有什麼鮮事？

句型解說

美國人見面，打招呼寒暄，一般是用以下幾句：

① How are you?

② How are you doing?

③ How do you do?

除了以上三句，你有沒有聽過一見面就打招呼說：

Hey. What's up? 注意這一句話是最流行招呼語，比以上三句都酷，特別用在熟朋友之間，倍覺親切。

舉一反三

除了 What's up? 以外，以下三句也是最流行的招呼語。
在朋友之間，儘管用，保證是最酷的招呼。

類似用語　　① What's going down?
　　　　　　② What's new?
　　　　　　③ What's shaking?

靈活運用

1. John: **Hi, Mary. What's up?**
　　　　嗨，瑪麗，有什麼鮮事嗎？

　【說明】 What's up? 如果不是用在剛見面時的打招呼，就是
　　　　表示問對方發生了什麼事。這樣的用法，與 What's
　　　　happening?；What's going on? 意思相同。

　Mary: **Nothing much.**
　　　　沒什麼。

　　　　What's new with you?
　　　　你有什麼鮮事嗎？

2. John: **Hi, Mary. What's new?**
　　　　嗨，瑪麗，有什麼鮮事嗎？

　Mary: **Nothing much.**
　　　　沒什麼。

　　　　How about you?
　　　　那你呢？

3. **You look pretty sad. What's up?**
　　你看起來很悲傷，怎麼啦？

2

Hey, Give me five.

嗨，好啊！

Hey, give me five.

"Hey, Tom! Give me five!" shouted Henry, raising his hand.

"嗨，湯姆！好啊！亨利大叫著，並把手舉起來。

句型解說

在現代美國電影或電視中，常常可看到兩個人手伸出來互相拍掌，這種現象發生在兩人初見面時，或是有什麼值得兩人高興的事發生時。有時會說 Give me five. 有時兩人很有默契時，不說 Give me five. 就互相擊掌。

Tom: **Hey, dude!　Give me five!**
嗨，傢伙，好啊！。

John: **How are you doing, Tom?**
湯姆，你好嗎？

I haven't seen you since last winter.
自從去年冬天以後就沒見過你了。

美國簡介

面　積：9,363,400 平方公里　　國鳥：白頭鷹

國　花：玫瑰　　　　　　　　　　首都：華盛頓特區

國慶日：七月四日　　　　　　　第一大城：紐約

國　旗：星條旗

美國熱狗（Hot Dog）

　　美國人是大而化之的民族，連他們的飲食習慣也不例外！賣熱狗的小販在美國隨處可見，像是電影院、鬧區、遊樂場…各個大街小巷，都有物美價廉、讓美國人愛不釋口的 Hog Dog，就像台灣的熱門小吃－香雞排，只是台灣人比美國人更幸福，因為除了雞排，還可以配上一杯香香 QQ 的珍珠奶茶呢！

Pissed off
很生氣

You look very pissed off about something.
什麼事惹你生氣了。

句型解說

　　piss 這個字，本身的意思是小便。pissed off 這個片語卻表示很生氣，它不是源於 piss（小便）的意思。但因為同字，很多人以為 pissed off 的用法不雅。不過，儘管有人認為不雅，用 pissed off 來表示生氣卻是很流行的說法。不管是在公共場合，電視或電台裡都可隨時聽到。

　　為了表示你跟得上時代，下次說不高興時，別再用 angry 這個字，太落伍了。切記用 pissed off。

類似用語：ticked off

靈活運用

1. She's always pissed off about something.
   她總是愛為某些事生悶氣。

2. Man, is that guy pissed off!
   唉呀，那傢伙真的很生氣。

3. I was pissed when I found out I was not invited to her birthday party.
   當我發現她沒有邀我去她的生日宴會時，我很生氣。
   【說明】注意，這裡用 pissed 而不用 pissed off，意思一樣。

4. I'm really ticked off at her!
   我真的對她很生氣。

5. You look really pissed off. What's up?
   你好像很不高興。怎麼啦？

Get out of my face.

閃遠一點，別煩我

Get out of my face. I've had enough of you.

閃遠一點，別煩我。我受夠你了。

句型解說

　　Get out of my face. 這句話一聽就有很濃的火藥味，這句話是當一個人很煩時，對週遭想與他說話的人怒吼出來的氣話。當你說出這句話時，旁邊的人都會知道你的心情真的很不好。

舉一反三

Get out of my face. 較溫和的說法是 Leave me alone.

靈活運用

1. John: **Mary, are you O.K.?**
瑪麗，你還好嗎？

Mary: **Get out of my face.**
閃遠一點，別煩我。

John: **Chill! What's up with you?**
幹嘛！你怎麼啦？

2. John: **Mary, you look so down.**
瑪麗，你看起來很沮喪。
What's up?
怎麼了？

Mary: **Get out of my face.**
閃遠一點，別煩我。
I hate you all.
我恨你們每一個人。
Nobody cares about me.
沒有人關心我。

美國人的流行文化

美國倡導個人主義，強烈地表現自我，在服飾打扮上也是如此。尤其是美國的年輕人，喜歡追求新奇、酷愛標新立異，所以美國女性常以活潑、性感的服飾表現出自己的線條美，而男生則傾向以運動、有型的穿著，表現出陽剛的男人味！

Chill out!

別煩躁！冷靜點！

Don't be so upset! Chill out!

別這麼生氣，冷靜點。

句型解說

　　Chill out! 是時下年輕人常掛在嘴邊的話，不太高興看到某人，或別人講的話不太中聽，你都可以回他一句 Chill out! 或 Chill! 這句話雖然原本的意思是叫人家冷靜點，別煩躁，但使用時也有「幹嘛」的意思。

舉一反三

Chill out! 是流行的用語；Calm down 則是較古板的用語。

類似用語：keep one's cool.

相反用語：lose one's cool. 失去冷靜。

　　　　　freak out 發脾氣。

靈活運用

1. Mary: **I can't stand her anymore.**

   我實在受不了她。

   She's really a jerk.

   真是一個討厭鬼。

   John: **Chill out!**

   冷靜點。

2. Mary: **Who the heck do you think you are?**

   你以為你是什麼人？

   John: **Chill!**

   神氣什麼！

美國的民族

　　你心目中的美國人是怎樣的呢？美國的社會學家 Marvin Baron 認為，大部份美國人的個性傾向獨立自主，而且他們個性積極認真、努力工作。美國人的行事風格率直開朗，也喜歡助人為善，但是一般而言，他們的說話做事通常也較直接、不會拐彎抹角！

MP3-7

Bomb

搞雜了

I bombed my final.

我的期末考考壞了。

句型解說

在這裡 bomb 這個字是當動詞用，意思是搞砸了，一般來說，我們在課本上所學的，當動詞是爆炸，當名詞是炸彈。這個字美國人目前用來做別的意思，當動詞指搞砸了，當名詞指很差的演出。當你聽到美國人說 The show was a real bomb.

你可要知道他說的不是炸彈，而是說演出很差勁。就像美國人說某樣東西很不好時，用 lemon 這個字一樣。

舉一反三

類似用語：blow.

靈活運用

1. Mother: **How was your test?**
   你考得怎樣？

   John: **I bombed it.**
   我考得很差。

   Mother: **Don't worry. I am sure you made a good grade.**
   別擔心，我相信你一定能得到好成績。

2. **I think I blew my math test.**
   我想，我的數學考得很差。

3. Tom: **How was your performance?**
   你的表演怎麼樣？

   Mary: **I blew it.**
   我演得不好。

Freak out

大發脾氣

Stop bugging him. He's gonna freak.

別再煩他了，他快要發脾氣了。

句型解說

　　大發脾氣，用 freak out 或 freak 都行。這個意思的老式說法是 be very upset，但美國現在年輕人，卻開口閉口都用 freak 或 freak out，很少在年輕人的對話中，聽到 be very upset。

舉一反三

相反用語：keep one's cool.

例： My mom kept her cool when I told her I

failed my math.

當我告訴她，我的數學不及格時，我媽竟然沒有發脾氣。

1. If he doesn't arrive in five minutes, I'm going to freak.

5 分鐘之內他還不來的話，我就要發火了。

2. I am going to freak out if he doesn't knock it off.

如果他再不停止的話，我會大發脾氣。

3. I bombed my final, now my parents are going to freak out.

我的期末考考壞了，我的父母一定會大發脾氣。

4. When Jenny came home after midnight, her mother freaked out.

當珍妮半夜才回家時，她媽媽大發脾氣。

Flip out

嚇呆了；抓狂

My mother flipped when she saw my new haircut.

當我媽媽看到我的新髮型時，她簡直要抓狂。

句型解說

flip 這個字原本指翻東西的意思，引申為嚇呆了或抓狂，是時下美國年輕人流行的說法。可用 flip 或 flip out 都可以。

靈活運用

1. My mother flipped when I told her I failed my math.

   當我告訴我媽媽，我的數學不及格時，她簡直要抓狂。

2. You'll flip out when I tell you what happened last night.

   當你聽到我告訴你昨晚發生的事時，你一定會抓狂。

Top

9

MP3-10

Knock it off

停止

Could you please knock it off?
可不可以請你停止？

句型解說

　　Knock it off 的意思就是 stop，用 stop 可以說是簡單明瞭，但用 knock it off 則更酷。

　　類似用語：hold it.

靈活運用

1. **Could you please knock it off?**
   可不可以請你停止。

Your crying is driving me crazy.

你的哭聲快把我逼瘋了。

2. If you don't knock it off, I'll beat you up real bad.

如果你再不停止的話，我會好好地揍你一頓。

3. You'd better knock it off.

你最好停止。

Or he's gonna freak.

否則他會大發脾氣。

美國的節慶：感恩節

　　每年 11 月的第四個星期四是感恩節，源於西元 1621 年，清教徒至麻州傳教時，在嚴寒的冬天，沒有食物可吃，幸而印第安人教他們如何種植玉米，讓他們免於飢餓。所以，感恩節的傳統習俗就是要吃大餐（烤火雞、紅莓醬、馬鈴薯、南　派），並且和至親好友團聚，感謝彼此的照顧。

Top 10

MP3-11

Drives me nuts

把我逼瘋了

She keeps nagging at me.
It really drives me nuts.

她一直對我嘮叨不停,快把我逼瘋了。

句型解說

當遇到某些情況,真夠煩、都快把人逼瘋了。可以説 drive me nuts,nuts 這個字就是腦筋不正常的意思。nag 就是嘮叨不停。

舉一反三

類似用語:drive me crazy.

靈活運用

1. That noise is driving me crazy.
   那個噪音快把我逼瘋了。

2. Stop crying. It is driving me crazy.
   不要哭了,我快發瘋了。

Cut class

蹺課

She keeps cutting class.

她總是蹺課。

句型解說

蹺課，最常用的説法就是 cut class。

靈活運用

1. If she keeps cutting class, she'll fail the course.

   如果她繼續蹺課的話，她那科就會被當掉。

2. I can't cut that class, I've missed too much already.
我不能再蹺課了，我缺課太多了。

會話練習

John: You look really pissed off.
你好像很生氣。

What's up?
怎麼了？

Mary: Get out of my face, would you?
閃遠一點，別煩我，好嗎？

John: Chill out! What's up with you, anyway?
幹嘛，誰惹你啦？

Mary: I'm sorry. It's just that I bombed my math exam and now my father is going to freak out.
對不起，只是我數學考差了，我爸爸一定會大發脾氣。

Chapter

Give me a break

別開玩笑了！

Oh, come on. Give me a break.
噢，算了吧，別開玩笑了！

句型解說

　　Give me a break 是一句很流行的話，舉凡你聽到別人說一個消息、一件事或任何一句話，你聽了不相信，都可回他一句 Give me a break，既清楚表達你不相信他說的話，而且又充分地運用了一句流行的英語。Give me a break 和 Get out of here 這兩句話都有你不相信對方的意思，但 Get out of here 所表達的不相信中，含有興奮的意味在。

　　例如，有人說你很漂亮，你回答他說：「別騙了」，

要用 Get out of here，而不用 Get me a break。因為別人説你漂亮，你雖説別開玩笑了，事實上卻芳心暗喜呢。

靈活運用

1. Mary: Do you know who is going with John?
   你知道誰是約翰的女朋友嗎？

   Jack: Ann Lee?　Give me a break. She's such a snob.
   李安妮嗎？別開玩笑了，那個大騷包。

2. John: Tell you what.
   告訴你一個消息。

   I'm going to beat Tom at math contest.
   我會在數學比賽中贏湯姆。

   Mary: Oh, give me a break.
   別開玩笑了。

   Tom is so good at math.
   湯姆的數學那麼好。

   Nobody is going to beat him.
   沒有人能贏他的。

Get out of here!

別騙了！別開玩笑了！

Get out of here!

John: You are very pretty.
你好漂亮。
Mary: Get out of here.
別騙了！

句型解說

Get out of here! 原本的意思是走開，但現在卻演變成「別騙了」這個完全不同的意思。這個別騙了的用法非常流行，你在美國的電影、電視裡常可聽到。

例如在「黃金女郎」劇中，有位英俊的男士對其中的一位女郎說「妳很漂亮」，她回答說：「Get out of here.」這個男士竟然真的走了出去，害得她不知該如何才

好。當然,這是喜劇,搏君一笑,美國人不會聽不懂這裡的 Get out of here! 是「別騙了」的意思。

　　Get out of here!,除了有「別開玩笑」的意思外,也常用來表示「絕對不是」,Absolutely not! 到底應做什麼樣的解釋,看上下文的意思,就可明白了。

靈活運用

1. John: I've just heard that Tom got laid off.
   我剛聽說湯姆被解僱了。

   Mary: Get out of here!
   別開玩笑了。

2. John: Is that your boy friend?
   那是你男朋友嗎?

   Mary: Get out of here!
   絕對不是!

美國的節慶:美國獨立紀念日

　　7 月 4 日是美國獨立紀念日,也就是美國的國慶日,美國人在當天會舉行國慶遊行、野餐、夜間音樂會,煙火,掛上美麗的星條旗,旗海飄揚、普天同慶。

Kiss up to

拍馬屁，巴結

She's just kissing up to the teacher, so she'll get a good grade on that paper.

她就是愛拍老師的馬屁，所以她的報告可以得到好成績。

句型解說

kiss up to 是說為了某種目的去討好某人，後面通常接人。

1. Mary   She keeps cutting class.
   她那堂課總是蹺課。

   How can she ace the course?
   怎麼可能拿到高分呢？

   Tom   Because she kissed up to the teacher.
   因為她拍老師的馬屁。

2. She's just kissing up to her boss, hoping she'll get a promotion.
   她就是拍她老闆的馬屁，希望能升官。

美國的節慶：總統節

　　美國人很有趣，把 2 月的第三個禮拜一訂為總統節，目的是可以「同時」慶祝二位偉大的總統。第一位是在 2 月 22 日誕生的美國國父－喬治・華盛頓；另一位則是在 2 月 12 日誕生，解放黑奴、統一南北的林肯總統。

Ace a test

考得很好

MP3-16

I aced my math final this afternoon.
我今天下午的數學期末考，考得不錯。

句型解說

　　ace 這個字是年輕人和大學生流行詞語，說考試考得很好，或某件事做得很好。

靈活運用

Mary: **How did your English test go?**
你的英文考得如何？

Tom: **I aced it.**
我考得很好。

16

Go with someone

與固定的人約會

Do you know who's going with John?

你知道誰是約翰的女朋友嗎?

句型解說

某人 go with 某人,表示這兩人是固定的異性朋友。另一說法是他們兩人 go together。他們兩人是固定的男女朋友,也可以用 They are dating。

舉一反三

類似用語:be dating, go together.

1. Mary: How long have you and Jenny been going together?

   你和珍妮約會多久了？

   John: I've been going with her since last June.

   我從去年 6 月就開始她在一起。

2. How long have you and Jenny been dating?

   你和珍妮約會多久了？

3. They are dating each other exclusively.

   他們是固定的男女朋友。

A friend is easier lost than found.

失去朋友比交朋友還容易

Have a crush on someone

愛上某人

Jenny thinks she has a crush on Tom.

珍妮認為她愛上湯姆了。

句型解說

　　年輕人在一起，某人愛上某人是常見的新聞，以前的說法是 fall in love with，現在的年輕人不再用這種說法了。他們用 have a crush on someone。注意聽美國年輕人說話，你就可常聽到某人 has a crush on 某人。

類似句型：be interested in

1. Jenny says she'll never have a crush on anyone again.
   珍妮說，她不會再愛上任何人了。

2. John has a crush on Mary.
   約翰愛上瑪麗。

3. Tom is interested in Mary.
   湯姆對瑪麗有興趣。

4. John stole my high school sweetheart from me.
   約翰搶走我高中時代的女朋友。

美國的節慶：新年

　　美國新年是在國曆的 1 月 1 日，美國人在 12 月 31 日晚上就會群聚狂歡，並且希望在新的一年裡，可以事事順利、天天開心！

Be crazy about
為之瘋狂，愛上

Boys are crazy about her.
男孩們為她瘋狂。

句型解說

男孩子為她瘋狂，就是男孩子很迷她，很愛她。

舉一反三

類似用語：

have crush on~

have the hearts for~

head over heels in love with~

1. He is crazy about the new girl.
   他愛上了新來的女孩子。

2. He has crush on her.
   她愛上她。

3. If you have a crush on her, why don't you tell her?
   如果你愛上她，何不告訴她？

4. I know you have the hearts for her.
   我知道你愛上她了。

5. Tom was head over heels in love with her.
   湯姆真的愛上她。

Head over heels

從頭到腳，完全地

CHAPTER 2

She was head over heels in love with the rock star.

她真的迷上那搖滾樂明星。

句型解說

　　head 是頭，heel 是腳跟，head over heels，從頭到腳，從頭到腳，指的是完全的。常常跟 in love with ～ 連用，說真正地愛上某人；或跟 in love 連用，說兩人真正地相愛。

1. **John is head over heels in love with Mary.**

   約翰真心地愛上瑪麗。

2. **They are head over heels in love.**

   他們是真心相愛。

美國的觀光景點：紐約（New York）

　　紐約是美國第一大城，其重要性，甚至常常讓人誤以為她就是美國的首都。紐約又叫大蘋果（Big Apple），也是是美國商業、媒體大眾傳播的中心。她分為 5 個區域：曼哈頓（Manhattan）、皇后（Queens）、布魯克林（Brooklyn）、布朗（The Bronx）以及李奇文（Richmond）。

　　紐約市人文薈萃，代表當代藝術的博物館頗多，像是：古根漢博物館（Guggenheim Museum）、現代藝術博物館（The Museum of Modern Art）、大都會博物館（Metropolitan Museum of Art）…還有著名的建築物及景點：自由女神像（Statue of Liberty）、帝國大廈（Empire State Building）、布魯克林大橋（Brooklyn Bridge）、時報廣場（Time Square）…觀光資源十分豐富！

20

MP3-21

Flit around

滿場飛

Whenever she is at a party. She's always flitting around.

每當她參加宴會，總是喜歡滿場飛。

句型解說

在任何場合或是宴會，你總是會看到滿場飛的花蝴蝶，你知道美國人怎麼說嗎？就是 flit around。

靈活運用

Do you know that girl flitting around at the party last night?

你認不認識昨晚在宴會上像花蝴蝶的那個女孩？

Flirt with

送秋波；眉來眼去

Jenny always flirts with men she meets at bars.

珍妮總在酒吧對男人眉來眼去的。

句型解說

　　flirt 這個字是說用眉目傳情，後面通常要加 with 這個介係詞，是一般美國人常用的字，不管任何年紀的人說到某人用眼睛去勾搭、傳情都用 flirt with。

1. John is flirting with Mary.
   約翰正用眉目向瑪麗傳情。

2. Steven Spielberg has been flirting with Oscar awards for many years.
   史蒂芬史匹柏幾年來一直對奧斯卡金像獎頻送秋波。

CHAPTER 2

如何和美國人做朋友

　　美國人是很有冒險、積極進取的精神，他們非常重視工作及個人表現，和東方人謙虛保守、不善表達的文化大異其趣。所以和美國人在一起時，可以學會他們率直敢言、勇於表達真實自我的美式精神！

　　美國人雖然喜歡社交，但他們相當重視個人隱私，所以在初識美國朋友時，儘量不要過問關於他的家庭、收入、宗教、或政治等較私密的問題。另外，美國人喜歡正直、守時的人，和美國人互　時，有誠實的態度是很重要的！

Flirt

騷婆娘，騷貨

She's the biggest flirt in school.
她是全校最騷包的女孩子。
She keeps flirting with boys.
她總是愛跟男孩子拋媚眼。

句型解說

　　flirt 這個字當動詞用時，指拋媚眼、送秋波、眉來眼去。當名詞用時，指喜歡到處勾搭的人。另外有兩個字也常用來形容愛招搖、愛出鋒頭的女孩子。但卻表達了不同的意思。snob 指喜歡穿戴的很漂亮，到處招搖的女孩子。airhead 則是指只是漂亮卻沒有腦筋的花瓶。

舉一反三

類似用語：snob, airhead

靈活運用

1. The new girl is such a flirt.
   新來的女孩子很騷包。

2. She is too much of an airhead to be school president.
   她呀花瓶一個，不能做學生會會長。

3. She's such a snob. I don't like her.
   她太愛招搖了。我不喜歡她。

入境美國時要注意什麼

　　通關入境美國時，像是肉類食品（包括肉鬆、肉乾等）以及生鮮蔬果等動、植物是禁止攜帶入境的。另外，某些特定的項目在入境時也需要申報；所攜的物品如果超過一定的限額，也必須繳稅。

Gag me!

真令我噁心！

Did you see that Jenny was flirting with the men at the party?
That gags me.

你有沒有看到珍妮一直在對宴會上的男人拋媚眼？
真噁心！

句型解說

　　談話中有時談到某些情況，我們會說「真噁心」！表示對所發生的情形很厭惡。正式的說法是「That makes me sick.」，但年輕人不用「That makes me sick.」這個句子，而用「Gag me!」，簡單明瞭又傳神。這個用法是時下美國年輕人尤其是女孩子常掛在嘴邊的話，每遇到

某一情況，不太喜歡時。Gag me! 兩字就出口了。另外一個字：Gross！也是在遇到不喜歡的情況時，常用的一個字。

靈活運用

1. **Gag me!　Jenny and Tom are going together.**
   真噁心！珍妮和湯姆在約會呢！

2. **Mary is dating a married man. Gag me!**
   瑪麗和一個有婦之夫約會，真噁心。

3. **School's hamburgers gross me out.**
   學校的漢堡真難吃。

◀美國克萊斯勒大樓
（Chrysler Building）。

Totally
真的很～

That rock band is totally hot.
那個搖滾樂團真的很受歡迎。

句型解說

　　total 和 totally 是年輕人流行的用語，用在強調所形容的東西或加強一個形容詞的意思。

靈活運用

1. **What a total jerk he is!**
   他實在是個十足的混蛋！

2. She's totally nasty.
她真的很騷包。

会話練習

Mary:	Do you know who's going with John? 你知不知道約翰的女朋友是誰？
Jenny:	Cathy Lin? Give me a break. She's such a snob. 凱茜林嗎？她是那麼愛招搖的人
Mary:	But John has a mad crush on her. 但約翰是真的愛上她了。
Jenny:	Get out of here. 別開玩笑了。
Mary:	I'm dead serious. She always wears heavy makeup and flits around all the time. 我是說真的。她總是化著濃粧，一天到晚到處騷包。
	Boys are really crazy about her. 男孩子很為她著迷的。
Jenny:	Oh, gag me! She's totally nasty. 噢，真噁心！她實在是個騷貨！

Chapter

You can say that again.

你說對了！

Mary: What's going on?

怎麼了？

You look stressed.

你看起來快崩潰了。

Tom: You can say that again.

你說對了。

I stayed up late three nights
in a row.

我連續三個晚上都在熬夜。

句型解說

　　You can say that again. 這句話按照字面翻譯是

「你可以再說一遍，但事實上，這是一句美國人常用的句子，尤其用在熟朋友之間，表示同意對方的説法。也可以説 That's very true! 但在熟朋友之間用 You can say that again. 就顯得俏皮多了。

靈活運用

Tom: Your dress is the latest style.
你的洋裝是最新的款式。

You have good taste.
你的品味真好。

Mary: You can say that again.
你説對了。

I bought it in Paris last week.
我上禮拜在巴黎買的。

灰狗巴士（Greyhound）

美國地大物博、幅員遼闊，公路網遍佈全國。灰狗巴士（Greyhound Bus）提供美國各城市間的交通服務。由於它班次很多、往來頻繁，通常也選在夜間發車，並且價位便宜，所以頗受美國平民或世界各地遊客的青睞。

想去美國自助旅行的朋友，可以上網預訂車票，享受灰狗巴士方便、平價的服務！

In a row
連續的

You have been late for work three days in a row.
你已經連續三天上班遲到了。

句型解說

　　in a row 指連續的，這個字跟 continuous 不一樣的用法，是説一個接著一個。例如説一連幾天或一連幾夜。

靈活運用

1. I stayed up late three nights in a row.
   我一連三個晚上都在熬夜。

2. He won the best actor award four years in a row.
   他連續四年贏得最佳男主角獎。

27

I'll say.

我也有同感。

Tom: She's such a doll.
她真的很可愛。

John: I'll say.
我也有同感。

句型解說

　　在用英文聊天時，有時會覺得不知該如何接下去，記住這些簡單的句子，聊起來時不僅順口，又貼切。

　　例如，對方說了一件事情，你很有同感，別老是Yes，Yes，I think so. 用 I'll say. 表示如果由我來說，我也會這樣說。或是 You said it.，我要說的，你剛才已經說了，都是表示同意對方的說法，這兩句話都是很流行的用語，只要場合對了，儘管用。

CHAPTER 3

類似用語：You said it.

1. Tom: What a handsome couple they make!

    他們真是天生的一對。

    Mary: I'll say.

    是啊！我也有同感。

2. Tom: This test is killing me.

    這次考試真難。

    Mary: You said it.

    是啊！我也這麼想。

    I'm afraid I'll fail the course.

    我怕我這科會不及格。

美國名人語錄

「當你成功時，幾乎每個人都會站在你這邊；但在你做錯事受責備時，只有真正的朋友會站在你身旁。」

28

Fall apart

崩潰；解散

When she learned of her mother's death, she fell apart.
當她聽到她母親的死訊時，她整個人都崩潰了。

句型解說

To fall apart 本來的意思是東西解體，或者是一個團體解散的意思，若用來指人的情緒的話，就是指一個人情緒受不了，要崩潰了。

靈活運用

1. This old car is about to fall apart. You'd better sell it.
   這部老爺車都快解體了。你最好把它賣了。

2. What happened to you?
   你怎麼啦？
   You look like you're gonna fall apart.
   你看起來好像要崩潰了。

Fed up

無法再忍受

Stop whinning, I'm fed up.
別哭了，我受不了了。

句型解說

　　Be fed up 不只是生氣，而且是已經忍耐到極限。不管是媽媽被小孩子吵得受不了、老師被學生吵，或者是工作場所，你都可以常聽到某人說他 fed up。此話一出，不僅表示生氣，還意味著受不了，下一波行動將會很激烈。

靈活運用

1. I'm fed up. If you don't knock it off this minute, I'll beat you up.
   我受不了了，如果你現在不停止的話，我就要揍人了。
2. I'm fed up with this work.
   這工作實在令我受不了。

Dump her / him

甩掉他 / 她

Mary dumped John to go with Peter.
瑪麗把約翰甩掉，開始跟彼得約會。

句型解說

　　To dump 這個字當動詞，是倒垃圾的意思。引伸到交朋友方面，年輕人常說的把某人甩掉，美國年輕人就用 dump, dump my girlfriend（甩掉女朋友）。但若不是說異性固定交往的朋友，而是用於普通朋友，那就不用 dump，而用 drop。Tom is dropped by a friend. 指一位朋友不和他做朋友了。

靈活運用

1. After 30 years, he dumped his wife.
   他在結婚 30 年後甩掉他的妻子。

2. Mary was dumped by her boy friend.
   瑪麗被她男朋友甩了。

CHAPTER 3

Break up

男女朋友吹了

Tom:	Are you going out with John tonight?
	你今晚要和約翰約會嗎？
Mary:	No, we broke up.
	沒有，我們吹了。

句型解說

　　在年輕人的談話中，常聽到某人跟她的男朋友吹了。美語中 break up 也是在年輕人談話中常用的字。另一種說法，不是吹了，而是兩人的關係淡了，to turn cold。如：Our friendship turns cold.（我們的友誼變淡了）。

1. I broke up with John.
   我和約翰吹了。

2. After being together for three years, they broke up.
   交往了三年後，他們吹了。

3. They fell in love at fist sight. But one month later, their relationship turned cold.
   他們一見鍾情，但過了一個月後，他們的感情變淡了。

CHAPTER 3

美國人的經濟觀

　　美國的經濟強國，建立於「消費」之上，而非「儲蓄」。美國人個性積極進取，但也重視物質享受。美國政府愛花錢，人民也愛花錢，這種觀念造就了美國人及時行樂的消費觀，這就是美國人的消費創造所得的理論。

　　美國廣闊的消費市場，大量繁衍美式企業，像是：微軟、麥當勞、可口可樂、福特汽車，同時透過新奇有趣、娛樂 強的美式廣告，產品暢行全球。

Are you kidding?

你在開玩笑嗎？

You call me a snob, are you kidding?
你說我下流，你在開什麼玩笑？

句型解說

　　在這裡這句話是表示不相信對方說的話。kid 的意思是小孩，用作動詞，Are you kidding? 字面意思是你在說小孩子的話嗎？也就是說，你在開玩笑嗎？

靈活運用

1. Mary: Are you going out tonight?
　　　　你今晚要出去嗎？

Tom: **Are you kidding?**
你開什麼玩笑？

I stayed up all night last night.
我昨晚整夜都沒睡。

2. Mary: **Didn't you just have breast enlargement?**
你是不是剛做過隆乳？

Jane: **Are you kidding?**
你開什麼玩笑？

What makes you think so?
你怎麼會這麼想呢？

Mary: **Well, I didn't know your figure is so great.**
嗯，我以前都不知道你的身材這麼棒！

美國人的體育文化

　　美國人積極、酷愛冒險，不只表現在社會、經濟上，比起其他國家，美國人對體育競賽更是樂此不疲，像是：美國棒球、美式足球、美國 NBA 職籃…美國人酷愛體育，除了他們好勝的天性外，也有追求感官的刺激、大眾媒體的炒作、培養體能適應緊張的工作、以及醫療費太貴等諸多原因。

CHAPTER 3

Hot

很搶手；很酷；很性感

She is the hottest girl in school.
她是全校最熱門的女孩。

**Hey. That motocycle is hot. Can I
have a ride?**
嗨！那輛摩托車夠酷。我能不能騎一下？

She is hot, isn't she?
她很動感，對不對？

句型解說

　　Hot 這個字，大家學過是熱的意思。說食物，我們可以說是很辣。但這個字還有其他的意思，根據情況，句子可有不同的用法。首先，我們說 hot 是很搶手，也可以說

很酷，注意「酷」是英文的 Cool，但 hot 也能表達同樣的意思。至於説一個女孩子很性感，也可以用 hot，所以在不同的情況下，大家説 hot，來表達不同的意思，彼此總能心領神會的。

1. Michale Jackson is the hottest rock star.
   麥邁可傑克森是最紅的搖滾樂歌星。

2. Hey, your sport car is hot.
   嗨，你的跑車很酷。

3. The chick over there is hot.
   那邊那女孩很動感。

4. L.A. Boys is one of the hottest singing groups.
   洛城三兄弟是最紅的熱門樂之一。

Mary: Hey, John. What's going on?
嗨，約翰，你怎麼啦？
You look like you're gonna fall apart.
你看起來好像快崩潰了。

John: You can say that again.

你説對了。

Jenny is always two hours late for our dates.

珍妮每次約會總是遲到兩小時。

That really bugs me.

我實在很煩。

Mary: If you're that fed up, just dump her.

如果你真那麼受不了她的話，何不甩了她。

John: Are you kidding?

你在開什麼玩笑？

She's the hottest girl in school.

她是全校最搶手的女孩子。

美國名人語錄

「如果説成功有什麼秘訣，那就是能夠找出他人的觀點，讓自己不只從本身的角度來看事物，也能從別人的角度替他們著想。」

~美國汽車大王：享利·福特

Chapter

Beats me.

我不知道。

Mary: How old do you think she is?
你認為她幾歲？

Tom: Beats me.
我不知道。

句型解說

別人問你一個問題或一件事，你不知道，這個回答大家都知道，就是「I don't know.」。但這樣的回答太老套了，一點都跟不上流行，說我不知道最流行的說法是 Beats me. 或 You got me.。注意 Beats 要加 s 是 Beats me.，而不是 Beat me.。因為前面有一個字 It 省略掉了。

1. Tom: **Will she come on time?**
   她會不會準時到？

   Mary: **Beats me.**
   我不知道。

2. Tom: **Who will win the best actress award?**
   誰會贏得最佳女主角獎？

   Mary: **Beats me.**
   我不知道。

▲美國火車頭。

What the heck is this?

這到底是什麼？

What the heck is this?

What the heck is this?

這到底是什麼？

句型解說

　　heck 這個字原來應該是 hell 這個字，hell 是地獄，有人不喜歡用 hell 這個字，就轉音到 heck。在英語裡面，很多話有些因為宗教的因素，例如 gosh，我的天啊，（是 god 這個字的轉音，Gee 是 Jesus 的轉音），或是字本身太俗，例如 shit。有些人會轉音唸成類似的音，但本身意思一樣。

　　hell 這個字加到句子裡面去，並沒有影響句子的原意，只是加重語氣，或是表達憤怒而已。當有人對別人非常生氣時，有時會說 Go to hell，下地獄去受罪吧！

1. What the heck did you do that for?
   你為什麼這麼做？

2. What the heck do you think you're doing?
   你以為你在做什麼？

3. Where the heck are you going?
   你到底要去那裡？

4. Who the heck do you think you are?
   你以為你是誰？

5. Go to hell. You, little jerk.
   去死吧！你這個小混蛋。

比爾・蓋茨教學生做人（1）

第一、生活是不公平的，要去適應它。

第二、世界並不會在意你的自尊，這世界指望你在自我感覺良好之前先要有所成就。

MP3-37

Stuff

東西

Look at this stuff, isn't it great?
看看這東西，它是不是很棒？

句型解說

　　stuff 這個字是美國人一天到晚用的字，它可以指一切好的、不好的東西，隨時都可以用 stuff 這個字。隨著句子可知道 stuff 不同的意思。

　　例如電視劇裡，一位男士看到他的女朋友和另一個女孩子談得十分高興，他問她「What are you talking about？」（你們在聊什麼？），她不想告訴他實際的內容，就回答他 stuff 一個字。表示她們在談一些東西。

stuff：這個字，當名詞時指東西。當動詞用時，指塞滿了東西。例如 I'm stuffed. 指我很飽了。跟 I am full. 同樣意思。

靈活運用

1. **How can you expect me to eat this stuff?**
   你怎能期望待我會吃這種東西？

2. **It's good stuff, isn't it?**
   那是好東西，不是嗎？

3. Mary:　**More soup?**
   　　　　還要一些湯嗎？

   Tom:　**No, thanks. I'm stuffed.**
   　　　　不，謝謝。我很飽了。

▲美國遊輪。

CHAPTER 4

MP3-38

Have a heart
有點良心；發發善心

Oh, have a heart.
Give me some help.
喂！發發善心，幫我一些忙吧！

句型解說

　　年輕人講話，常常說：「喂，有點良心，不要這樣，不要那樣」，英文就是 have a heart。

舉一反三

類似用語：have pity.

1. If Jenny had a heart.　She wouldn't have dumped him.
如果珍妮有點良心，她不會把他甩掉。

2. Oh, have a heart.　Loan me ten bucks.
喂！發發善心吧！借我 10 塊錢。

3. Tom:　Why are you going with her?
你為什麼跟她在一起？

　　　She is not your type.
她跟你不同類型。

　　　She's a real airhead.
她只是一個花瓶。

John:　Have pity, Tom.
有點同情心，湯姆。

　　　I'm only a lonely, middle-aged bachelor.
我只是一個寂寞的中年單身漢。

CHAPTER 4

Just go for it

放手去做

Set up a goal. And just go for it.
定好目標，然後放手去做。

句型解說

Just go for it. 是一句鼓勵的話，遇到有人猶豫不決，或是不確定時，給他一句 Just go for it.，把一切疑慮都掃開。

靈活運用

1. **Don't worry and just go for it.**
   別擔心，儘管去做。

2. The plan sounds good.　Just go for it.
這個計劃聽起來不錯，放手去做吧！

3. Tom:　　I am interested in Mary.
我對瑪麗有興趣。

What do you think of her?
你覺得她怎麼樣？

Mr. Smith: She is a nice girl.
她是個好女孩。

If you like her, just go for it.
如果你喜歡她，儘管去追吧！

▲美國的車水馬龍。

Gross

真噁心

What's this stuff?　It looks gross.

這是什麼東西?看起來真噁心。

句型解說

　　gross 這個字,跟 gag 一樣,是美國年輕人一天到晚掛在嘴邊的話。不管是看到不喜歡的東西,或是某人令人討厭,某件事令人不悅,不是用 gross,就是用 gag。

　　gross 這個字還可以加上受詞,說 gross me out 就是 make me sick 或是 gag me,令我噁心的意思。

1. Tom: **You want to try this?**
   你要不要嚐嚐這個？

   Mary: **Yuck, what is this stuff?**
   唉呀，這是什麼東西。
   It looks gross.
   看起來真噁心。

   【說明】yuck 這個字，也是常聽到表示厭惡的說法。

2. **Look at that picture.**
   看看那張圖。

   Doesn't it gross you out?
   會不會令你噁心？

3. (Tom and John shake hands.)
   Mary: (to Tom) **Gross. You actually shook hands with him.**
   真噁心，你真的跟他握手。

   How could you put your hand against his?
   你怎麼會把手放到他手上。

   He is gay.
   他是個同性戀者。

40

MP3-41

Dude
老哥；老兄

Hey, dude, look at that girl.
喂，看看那女孩。

句型解說

　　dude 這個字是年輕人之間，叫男性的朋友用的，跟 guy 同樣的意思，但 guy 的用法則不限於某個年齡階層，一般在熟朋友之間，叫男性時常用。

　　另外一種叫法 you guys，則是叫眼前的一群人，不管叫男性或女性都可以用。

靈活運用

1. Hey dude, you got a lighter?
喂，你有打火機嗎？

2. Hey, you guys! Pay attention.
   喂，大家注意！

3. Mary: Jane told me that you've been feeling down lately.
   珍告訴我你最近有點沮喪。

   Jessy: She what? Don't you guys have anything better to do than sit around gossiping about my personal problems?
   什麼？你們這些人除了坐在那兒講我私人的問題外，難道沒有其他事可做？

會話練習

Mike:	(to John)Hey, Dude, try this. 嗨！試試這個。
John:	What the heck is it? 這是什麼？
Mary:	Beats me.　But it looks like good stuff. 我不知道，但是看起來還不錯。
	Just go for it. 放心吃吧！
John:	Yuck!　I'm not eating that. 我不吃那東西。
	It looks gross. 看起來很噁心。
Mary:	Oh, come on. 噢！算了。

Chapter

MP3-42

Get real

認清現實；別做夢了

When is he gonna get real and find a job?

他何時會認清現實，去找一份工作？

句型解說

在談話中，每遇到對方講的話不夠實際，我們常說要他 get real.（喂！別做夢了）。要對方說點實際一點的，別老是不切實際。

舉一反三

類似用語：Get a life.

1. You know you can't borrow her car.
   你知道你不可能向她借到車子。

   Get real.
   別做夢了。

2. You want to be a movie star.
   你要去做電影明星。

   Get real.
   別做夢了。

3. You have a crush on Mary.
   你愛上瑪麗。

   Get a life.
   別做夢了

美國名人語錄

「不要問你的國家可以為你做些什麼，要問你可以

為你的國家做些什麼。」

~美國總統：約翰・甘迺迪

Chick

女孩；馬子

Look at that chick over there.

看那邊那個女孩。

句型解說

　　用 chick 這個字說女孩子的時候，語氣中已有不尊重、輕佻的意思。一般說女孩用 girl。但在年輕人中，用字不喜歡老舊、古板，他們喜歡用 chick 這個字。注意這個字是男孩子用的字。

靈活運用

Did you know the chick flitting around at the party last night?

你認不認識昨晚在宴會上，那個滿場飛的女孩？

43

Man

哇塞！

Man, this test is tough.
哇塞，這次的考試真難。

句型解說

Man 這個字，是一個表示驚訝、感嘆的驚呼聲，不是說男人。所以，不管是男性，女性都可以用。

舉一反三

類似用語：" Boy!"

靈活運用

Man!　That blouse is drop-dead gorgeous.
哇塞！那件上衣簡直美極了。

Man!　This car is cool.
哇塞！這輛車子有夠酷。

No way!

免談

You think I'm going to sit around here while you're having fun at the party?

你以為我會乖乖待在這兒,而你卻在宴會玩樂?

No way!

免談。

句型解說

別人想要求你做什麼事,你若不喜歡,不必拐彎抹角的,乾脆一點,回他一句 No way.

John: **May I borrow your car?**
我可不可以借用你的車子？

Mary: **No way.**
免談。

John: **Will you please take this to the post office for me?**
可以請你幫我把這個帶去郵局嗎？

Mary: **No way.**
免談。

美國名人語錄

「具創造天性的人都有一個特徵，就是自信心特別
強。」

~美國心理學家：伊魯・何德

45

MP3-46

Have you lost it?

你瘋了？你阿達了嗎？

You want me to say sorry to her?
你要我去跟她道歉？

Have you lost it?
你瘋了？

句型解說

　　熟朋友之間，常遇到有人講話故意亂講，或是用舉止、動作在開玩笑。朋友常說你瘋了，或是你腦筋有沒有問題，這是一句無傷大雅的話，英語就是 Have you lost it?

舉一反三

類似用語：　Are you losing it?

You are losing it!

1. You want to ask Jessica out?
   你要與潔西卡約會嗎？

   Have you lost it?
   你瘋了。

   She's the biggest flirt in school.
   她是全校最騷包的女孩。

   She's gone out with practically every boy alive.
   幾乎每個男孩子都跟她有一手。

2. You have a crush on Charlie?
   妳愛上查理了嗎？

   Have you lost it?
   妳瘋了？

   Everybody knows he is gay.
   大家都知道他是同性戀。

John:	Hey, look! There's that chick Diane. 嗨！你看看！那就是那個叫黛安的女孩。 Man, she's a real beauty. 哇塞！她實在真漂亮。 Don't you think she's pretty? 你不認為她很漂亮嗎？
Tom:	No way! Have you lost it?

算了吧！你瘋了嗎？

She may have a good body.

她的身材不錯。

But as for her face, it's really ugly.

但她的臉有夠醜。

Get real!

看清楚一點！

美國的觀光景點：舊金山（San Francisco）

　　舊金山曾是從前中國廣東的老祖先，懷著一夜致富的夢想，遠度重洋來淘金的「金山」，迷人的 San Francisco！舊金山也是美西的金融中心，重要華埠區，因為臨著太平洋，所以也成為美國對亞洲貿易的重要港口之一。

　　舊金山也是個美麗的城市，最具代表性的景點，就是象徵當地地標的金門大橋（Golden Gate Bridge），那兒的斜陽落日，美不勝收！

Chapter

MP3-47

Rip-off

敲竹槓

Eight thousand bucks for that blouse is a rip-off.

那件上衣賣八千元，簡直是敲竹槓。

句型解說

　　rip-off 這個字，在美國人的談話中隨時可聽到，不管是買東西，上餐廳吃飯，或是請人修理東西，只要有人覺得太貴了。記得，用 It's too expensive. 的說法太落伍了。要說 It's a rip-off.。rip off 也可以當動詞用，就是敲竹槓。

Mary: **They'll charge 5,000 bucks to repair the oven.**
他們修理烤箱要收五仟元。
It's a rip-off.
簡直是敲竹槓。

John: **I didn't mean to rip you off.**
我並沒有要敲你竹槓。

美國名人語錄

「創造者有勇氣做與眾不同的事,不信任所謂的公式,不喜歡一成不變,喜歡跳出已經確立的某種秩序。」

~美國心理學家:慕尼

CHAPTER 6

Buck

元

Would you loan me ten bucks?

借我 10 塊錢好嗎？

I'm broke.

我身上一毛錢都都沒有。

句型解說

　　buck 是錢的意思，也就是國中學過的 dollar（元），但美國人偏愛說 buck。五塊錢說「five bucks」，二十元說「twenty bucks」。跟 five dollars、twenty dollars 的意思一樣，卻是更常用的。big bucks 指大錢，例如有人想賺大錢 make big bucks.

1. Mary: **How much is it?**
   多少錢？

   Clerk: **Ten bucks.**
   十塊錢。

2. **My dream is to make big bucks.**
   我的夢想就是賺大錢。

比爾‧蓋茨教學生做人（2）

　　第三、剛畢業的你不會有年收入 40,000 美元，在你把這個職位和汽車爭到手之前，你不會成為一個公司的副總裁，並擁有一部裝有電話的汽車。

　　第四、如果你認為你的老師嚴厲，等你在老板手下做事時再這麼想，因為老板不像老師，有任期的限制。

Broke
沒錢；沒現金

Mary:　I'm broke.
　　　　我身上一毛錢都沒有。
John:　I can loan you ten bucks.
　　　　If that'll help.
　　　　如果你需要的話，我可以借你 10 塊錢。

句型解說

　　broke 這個字，原本指破產，但也可以說沒錢。這個沒錢又有兩種含意，一種是手頭真的很緊；另一種是指身上沒有現金。所以，當美國人說 I'm broke. 時，可能指他身上沒有現金，而不是說他真的破產了。

1. I can't afford that.
   我買不起。

   I'm broke.
   我手頭很緊。

2. I'm broke.
   我身上沒有現金。

   I'm going to get some cash.
   我要去領一些現金。

美國的觀光景點：洛杉磯（Los Angels）

　　美國洛杉磯絕對是暢遊美西時，不可錯過的景點之一。洛杉磯除了氣候溫和、風景怡人外，到了當地，更可以感受到一種輕鬆、無拘無束的開放氣息。洛杉磯好玩的地方很多，像是：迪士尼樂園、環球影城、比佛利山莊、好萊塢、聖塔莫尼卡海灘、洛杉磯市中心等地，是個可以代表美國活潑、新奇、有創意的城市喔！

Window

商店櫥窗

I love the sweater in that window.
我很喜歡那櫥窗裡的毛衣。

句型解說

window 這個字大家學過的是窗戶。但要注意場合，它也可以說是窗店的櫥窗。例如我們去逛街，只是看看，並不打算買，就是 window-shop。

靈活運用

1. It has become a fashion for stores to set up Christmas trees in the windows during Christmas.

   在聖誕節期間，商店在櫥窗擺聖誕樹變成一種流行。

2. Was that the blouse on display in the window?

   那是櫥窗裡展示的那件上衣嗎？

50

Drop-dead gorgeous
棒極了

I love that blouse.
我喜歡那件上衣。
It's drop-dead gorgeous.
它真是棒極了。

句型解說

　　drop-dead gorgeous 用來形容人時，是指很帥或很漂亮，形容東西時，是指很棒或很漂亮。

　　drop-dead 當動詞卻是罵人的話，當你恨極了一個人，告訴他 drop-dead，去死吧！跟 go to hell 同樣的表達了恨極了的說法。

1. Tom Cruise is drop-dead gorgeous.
   湯姆克魯斯真的很帥。

2. Did you see Mary's boyfriend?
   你有沒有看過瑪麗的男朋友？

   He is drop-dead gorgeous.
   簡直帥透了。

3. That dress is drop-dead gorgeous.
   那件洋裝真漂亮。

▲ 自由女神。

美國名人語錄

「沒有冒險的意志，幾乎就沒有成功的可能 。」

~美國創造 研究專家：德金斯

Holy cow!

我的天啊！

Holy cow!
How can you do such a thing?
我的天啊！你怎麼可以做這種事？

句型解說

　　在談話中，我們除了陳述事情外，還常常會加一些驚呼聲來使我們的談話更有聲有色。英語中常見的有 Man! Boy! Yike! Gosh!

　　Holy cow! 是表驚訝的驚呼聲。have a cow，卻是動詞，表示非常的生氣。

Don't have a cow. Mom! I just spilled a little orange juice. 意思是老媽別氣！我只是灑了一些柳橙汁而已。

1. Holy cow!　Her house is like a castle.
   我的天啊！她家好像古堡一樣。

2. Holy cow!　The test is really tough.
   我的天啊！這次的考試真難。

3. Holy cow!　The telephone bill is 8,000 dollars this month.
   我的天啊！這個月的電話費是八千塊。

4. Holy cow!
   我的天啊！

   What did you do to your hair?
   你怎麼搞你的頭髮了？

   I can hardly recognize you.
   我幾乎認不出你來。

52

Talk about...

那真是…

Talk about a rip-off.
那真是敲竹槓啊！

句型解說

Talk about.... 其實就是 That was a.... 的意思，但用 Talk about 則生動多了。

靈活運用

1. Talk about a lousy movie.　This is it.
   那真是一部大爛片。

2. Talk about a lemmon.　You have to see my car.

你應該看看我的車子，那才叫破。

3. Talk about drop-dead gorgeous guys, you have to see Mary's boyfriend.

你應該看看瑪麗的男朋友，那真是很棒的一個人。

美國名人語錄

讀書如果不能應用，那麼所讀的書就像廢紙一般

~美國總統　喬治・華盛頓

Hold it down

小聲點

Hold it down when the baby is sleeping.
嬰兒在睡覺的時候，要安靜點。

句型解說

　　hold it down 從字面意思就可以看出，是把音量放小的意思，也就是小聲點的意思。

靈活運用

1. Hold it down, or you'll wake up daddy.
   小聲點，否則你會把老爹吵醒。

2. When you are in the classroom, you'd better hold it down.
   在教室裡，你最好小聲點。

CHAPTER 6

117 ◄◄◄

MP3-55

In fashion
正流行

Your dress is in fashion.
你的洋裝是目前流行的款式。

句型解說

說到服飾的流行，用 in fashion。

舉一反三

類似用語：in style, fashionable.
相反用語：out of fashion, old-fashioned.

1. Miniskirts are in fashion again.
   迷你裙又在流行了。

2. Jelly shoes are no longer in fashion.
   膠鞋已不流行了。

3. Your dress is in fashion. You have good taste.
   你的洋裝是最時髦的。你真有品味。

4. The hairstyle in fashion is shoulder length style.
   現在流行的髮型是長度及肩。

5. Long hair for men was considered fashionable twenty years ago.
   二十年前，男人留長頭髮是一種流行。

6. Being late for dates is in fashion.
   約會遲到是一種流行。

Mary:　　Gee, look at that blouse in the window.
呀！看看櫥窗裡的那件上衣。
It's drop-dead gorgeous.
真是棒極了。

I've got to have it.
我一定要買它

Mary: Holy cow!　8,000 bucks.
我的天啊！八千塊！

Talk about a rip-off.
真是敲竹槓。

Jenny: Hold it down.
小聲點。

Let's just get going.
我們繼續走吧！

Mary: That really bugs me.
我真的很氣。

The blouse is in fashion.
那件上衣是最時髦的款式。

And it matches my new skirt beautifully.
而且，它很配我那件新裙子。

Jenny: Shut up!　Let's get out of here.
閉嘴！我們出去吧！

Chapter

Burned up

很生氣

I'm really burned up at him.
我真的很氣他。

句型解說

　　burned up 很生氣，是形容詞，very angry 的意思。
burn me up 是動詞，令我生氣。

靈活運用

1. I've never been so burned up in my
   life.
   我一生中還沒這麼生氣過。

2. My mom was really burned up when I came home late last night.
當我昨晚很晚才到家時，我媽真的很生氣。

3. His carelessness really burns me up.
他的 心大意實在令我很生氣。

美國的觀光景點：西雅圖（Seattle）

　　西雅圖位於美國西北部，是個靠海的城市。其中湖光山色、群峰相連，西雅圖水氣豐富、多雨霧，所以相對美國其他的城市，她更增添了幾許大自然的美！

　　西雅圖也有很多有趣的旅遊景點，只要買一本城市護照（City Express），就可以暢遊當地的太空針塔（Space Needle）、屋蘭動物園（Woodland Park Zoo）、海灣渡輪（Argosy Cruises Harbor Tour）等地…門票一本玩到底，十分適合想赴美自助旅行的朋友。

Bug
惹煩；惹惱

Go away. Stop bugging me.
走開，別煩我。

句型解說

　　bug 這個字，有三種常見的意思。第一是當動詞，表示煩人的意思。另外當名詞有兩種意思，第一是竊聽器，第二是電腦軟體裡的小錯誤。

舉一反三

　　相似用語：annoy, burn one up.

1. That noise really bugs me.
   那個噪音實在令我很煩。

2. She is always late for our dates.
   她約會總是遲到。

   It really bugs me.
   實在令我很生氣。

3. They found a bug under their conference table.
   他們在會議桌下面，發現一個竊聽器。

4. Version one of the software has a lot of bugs.
   這個軟體的第一版有很多錯誤。

   I hope version two has improved.
   我希望第二版已改進了。

5. People like that just burn me up.
   那種人實在很惹我生氣。

6. It burns me up to hear you say dirty jokes.
   聽到你講黃色笑話，很令我生氣。

Push someone's buttons
惹火對方

He knows what upset me and doesn't push the buttons.

他知道什麼事會令我生氣，所以他從不會故意惹我生氣。

句型解說

　　push someone's buttons 惹火對方，意即已知對方不喜歡的事，或是明知何事會令對方生氣，就故意去說、故意去做。

1. John's parents don't get along.

   約翰的父母相處得不好。

   They always try to push each other's buttons.

   他們總是伺機惹火對方。

2. My girlfriend will be pushing my buttons within minutes of her arrival.

   我的女朋友一見面，就故意惹我生氣。

美國的觀光景點：芝加哥（Chicago）

　　芝加哥是美國中部的大城之一，經濟活動十分活躍，有很多美國大企業的總部及期貨交易市場均設於此；芝加哥同時也是處理全球 1/3 農、工業產品買賣的重鎮。芝加哥的文化資源頗豐，有著名的管弦樂團、博物館、圖書館的文化中心，也有怡人的公園、森林綠地。此城也兼容世界各地人種，反映出多元豐富的文化。

Have a screw loose

腦筋不正常

The woman keeps murmuring over there all day long.

那邊那個女人，一天到晚喃喃自語。

I think she has a screw loose.

我想她腦筋大概有問題。

句型解説

　　have a screw loose 或 get a screw loose 可以指某人神智不太清楚。但若是朋友間聊天，則不是真的說對方腦筋不正常，而是指對方說的話你不中意，故意說對方 get a screw loose。

舉一反三

相似用語：lose it.

靈活運用

If you think I'd set foot in her house again, you've got a screw loose.

如果你認為我會再走進她家，你就是腦筋有問題。

A good beginning is half done.

好的開始是成功的一半。

59

It's on me.

我請客

Let's go out for dinner.

我們出去吃晚飯。

It's on me.

我請客。

句型解說

　　大家一起去吃飯、看電影等,你要出錢請客,就說 It's on me. 或 It's my treat.

舉一反三

類似用語： It's my treat.

　　　　　 Be my guest.

1. Let's go to a movie tonight.
   我們今晚去看電影。

   It's on me.
   我請客。

2. Tom:　I'd like this dinner to be my treat.
   今晚我請客。

   Mary:　No, no.　Let's each pay our own way.
   不，不，我們各付各的。

   Tom:　No, I really want to pay, because you've helped me so much.
   不，我是真的想請你，因為你幫我那麼多忙。

3. I'd like to buy you a lunch.
   我想請你吃中飯。

MP3-61

Set foot in somewhere
進入某地

> **If I were you, I wouldn't set foot in that store.**
> 如果我是你，我不會進那家商店。

句型解說

　　Set foot in somewhere，涉足某地、進入某地，這個用語，都用在否定句。表示你對那個地方很不滿意，你不會進那個地方，或其他理由，你不再去那個地方。

靈活運用

1. Not after the way she spoke to me.

在她那樣子對我説話以後。

I wouldn't set foot in her house!
我絕不會踏進她家一步。

2. I won't set foot in that restaurant again.
   我再也不去那家餐廳。

   The food is gross.
   它們的東西真難吃。

3. She joined in a health club. She went there everyday for three weeks, and then never set foot in the place again.
   她參加一個健身俱樂部，一連三個禮拜每天都去，然後就再沒去了。

Adversity makes a man wise, not rich.

逆境造就人才。

Yummy

很好吃；味道不錯

Oh, that cake is so yummy.

噢，那蛋糕真好吃。

句型解說

　　大家學過的英文，很好吃是 delicious。但各位在看美國電影、電視時，可能會常聽到 yummy 這個字。

靈活運用

1. The cookies in the window look so yummy.

櫥窗裡展示的餅乾看起來很好吃。

2. The fried chicken is yummy.
這炸雞味道不錯。

會話練習

John: How about going for a burger at "Burger Yummy."
要不要到那家叫「好吃漢堡」的店去吃漢堡？

Mary: No way!
免談！

If you think I'd ever set foot in that restaurant again.
如果你以為我會再去那家餐廳。

You've got a screw loose.
那你就是瘋了。

John: O.K. How about that one?
好吧！那邊那一家怎麼樣？

Mary: Oh, be serious.
噢！正經點。

That one is very expensive.
那家好貴喔！

John: Chill! It's on me.
別挑了！由我請客。

Chapter

Hello!

有沒有搞錯

I just got a job as a Japanese translator.
我剛找到日文翻譯的工作。
Hello! You don't speak Japanese.
有沒有搞錯！你根本不會說日語。

句型解說

　　Hello 這個字，大家都知道是美國人見面打招呼的話，在年輕人之間，卻演變出另外一個意思。例如：你覺得某人說出一句話，沒經過大腦隨便說說，或是心不在焉，好像在做白日夢，你就敲他的頭說「Hello, anybody home.」這句話問有沒有人在家，是指你清醒沒有的意思。Hello，在這兒的問法是說「你有沒有搞錯」。

舉一反三

類似用語：**Have you lost it?**

Top 63

MP3-64

Dough

錢

How much dough have you got?

你有多少錢？

句型解說

　　Money 是一個大家都知道的英文單字。但是在美國流行的詞語，不再說 money，而是說 dough，在美國的電影或電視中，美國人說 dough，你可知道，他們說的就是大家學過的 money 的意思。

靈活運用

1. I can't go to the movies tonight, I'm trying to save some dough.
   我今晚不能去看電影，我在想辦法存錢。

2. How much dough will it cost me?
   那要花我多少錢？

John
馬桶

I have got to run to the john.
我必須上廁所。

句型解說

　　我們現在用的抽水馬桶，是一位叫 John Crapper 的人發明的，所以沿用至今，john 指抽水馬桶，仍然是常用的說法。john 指馬桶，但用在句子裡，引申成廁所 。

舉一反三

類似用語：toilet, bathroom.

1. Tom is in the john.
   湯姆在廁所。

2. May I use your bathroom?
   我可不可以借用你的廁所？

3. It's your turn to clean the john.
   輪到你洗廁所了。

4. The john is stopped up.
   馬桶賭塞了。

▲美國街景一角。

Go to the bathroom

上廁所

Go to the bathroom

Tom went to the bathroom.

湯姆去上廁所。

句型解說

　　上廁所是每天必做的事，説到上廁所，中文有許多説法。英文也是一樣，有些是正式的説法，有些是常用的説法，有些是小孩子用的，有些是不雅的説法，一般在教科書中並沒有講清楚，你學了，用得不當，美國朋友都會替你臉紅。

　　你如果想上廁所，在人家家裡要用 bathroom 或 toilet，但用 bathroom 較好。在公共場所，常用的是 restroom。你也可以説 ladies' room, mens' room 或

powder room。但年輕人流行的說法用 john。小孩子的說法是 potty, girls' room 或 boys' room.

靈活運用

1. May I use your restroom?
   我可不可以借用你們的廁所？

2. Where is ladies' room?
   女廁所在那裡？

3. Tom is in the restroom.
   湯姆在廁所。

4. The restroom is over there.
   廁所在那裡。

美國的大眾文化

　　美國人相當重視知識的開發、資訊的流通、以及思想的傳播；所以像是報紙、雜誌、廣播、電視、電影等大眾媒體均十分發達，這不僅促使美國文化的大融合，發達的大眾媒體文化，更讓美國人敢言、敢說、敢秀的　格更為突顯。

Hit

大熱門；最搶眼；最搶手

You're going to be a hit at the party.
你會是宴會上最搶眼的人。

句型解說

　　hit 和 hot 的意思一樣，但 hit 是名詞，用法是某人、某首歌或某張唱片 is a hit。但 hot 是形容詞，用法是某人、某首歌 is hot。

靈活運用

1. My sister just wrote a book that I know

is going to be a hit.

我妹妹剛寫了一本書，我知道那本書一定會很搶手。

2. **This song is going to be a hit.**

這首歌一定會大受歡迎。

3. **Whitney Houston's latest album is a hit.**

惠妮休士頓的最新專輯很搶手。

比爾‧蓋茨教學生做人（3）

第五、如果你陷入困境，那不是你父母的過錯，所以不要抱怨，而是要從中記取教訓。

第六、在你出生之前，你的父母並非像他們現在這樣乏味。他們之所以變成今天這個樣子，是因為這些年來一直替你付帳單、幫你洗衣服、聽你自吹自擂。所以在對父母喋喋不休之前，還是先把你的房間整理乾淨吧。

Green

新手；沒經驗；菜鳥

If I were you, I wouldn't hire him.
如果我是你，我不會雇用他。
He's really green.
他一點經驗都沒有。

句型解說

我們說某人在某一行業裡是新手、沒經驗，或是在某人談話中，你覺得對方對某事很外行，都可以用 green 這個字來說。

靈活運用

I would rather be called green than pretend to be an old dog.
我寧願人家說我菜鳥，也不要裝老手。

Top 68

MP3-69

CHAPTER 8

Dirt

閒話;謠言

You've got any new dirt to tell me?
你有什麼新的消息要告訴我嗎?

句型解說

dirt 這個字本意是灰塵,但美國人常用來指 gossip,指大家傳來傳去的閒話或謠言。

靈活運用

1. What's the dirt on the new secretary in the manager's office?
   對於經理室新來的秘書,有什麼閒話嗎?

2. There's dirt on the affair between Jessica and the manger.
   關於潔西卡和經理之間的風流韻事,謠言滿天飛。

147

Dirty joke

黃色笑話

It's not nice to say dirty jokes when there are girls.

有女孩子在的場合,實在不宜說黃色笑話。

句型解說

講到黃色笑話,記得千萬別照字面翻,翻成 yellow joke,美國人聽到一定莫名其妙,不知道你在說什麼。

舉一反三

類似用語: talk dirty

toilet mouth

1. He likes to talk dirty.
   他喜歡講髒話。

2. Watch your toilet mouth.
   你髒話連篇，最好小心點。

3. I don't like to hear you say dirty jokes.
   我不喜歡聽你說黃色笑話。

美國的觀光景點： 拉斯維加斯（Las Vegas）

　　賭城拉斯維加斯，絕對是無人不知、無人不曉，她奇蹟似地被建立在內華達州荒涼的沙漠上，這個奇幻城市在過去只是個被黑幫控制的貪婪賭城，現在卻搖身一變，成為世界最有名的賭場及娛樂中心。

　　拉斯維加斯這個豪放的賭城，有全球最壯觀的飯店及賭場建築，像是米高梅（MGM Grand）、海市蜃樓（Mirage）、火鶴（Flamingo）、馬戲團（Circus Circus）、凱撒皇宮（Ceasar' Palace）…等等，當日幕低垂，這個不夜城就會穿上她五光十色的霓裳，向世人擺弄她最豔麗的舞姿！

Bullshit

鬼話連篇

Don't let him bullshit you.

別聽他鬼話連篇。

He doesn't know what he is talking about.

他不知道他自己在說什麼。

句型解說

bullshit 這個字，是由 bull 和 shit 二字合起來的，bull 是公牛，shit 是屎。合起來就是牛屎。bullshit 這個字非常流行，可當動詞，也可當名詞。

1. What he told you is a lot of bullshit.
他告訴你的，全是鬼話連篇。

Don't believe him.
別相信他。

2. Don't give me that bullshit.
別騙我了。

3. She didn't know the answers to any questions on the examination, so she just wrote a lot of bullshit.
這次考試的題目她都不會，只好亂寫一通。

4. You're full of bull.
你鬼扯，我才不相信你。

【說明】：在這個句型裡，用 bull 或 bullshit 都可以。

美國名人語錄

「想像比知識更重要。」

~美國物理學家：愛因斯坦

Cop

警察

Freeze, this is the police.

別　，這是警察。

句型解說

　　大家在課堂上學到的警察，英文是 policeman。但各位在美國影片裡，一定常聽到 cop 這個字。一般人叫警察 cop，但警察並不叫自己 cop，而說 police。

靈活運用

1. Don't drive so fast.
別開那麼快。

There's a cop.

那兒有個警察。

2. Some cops are headed this way.

有一些警察正向這邊走過來。

Freeze

別動

Freeze, or I'll shoot.
別動，否則我要開槍了。

句型解說

　　freeze 這個字，大家學過是冷凍的意思。但這個字卻有另外一個意思，是攸關生死的，大家不可不知道。當有人拿槍比著你，叫你別動時，就會大叫 freeze 。

　　這個用法，在美國的警匪片中常會出現，要保命不可不知此字！

1. Freeze, this is the police.

   別動，這是警察。

2. When someone calls "freeze", you'd better stand still, or you may get shot.

   當有人喊「別動」時，你最好站著別動，否則他會開槍打你。

會話練習

Mary: Tom is really annoying.

湯姆真的很煩。

He kept bugging me to loan him some dough.

他一直纏著我借他一些錢。

John: Get out of here.

別開玩笑了。

Tom's father is a millionaire, and he has to ask you for money?

湯姆的父親是個百萬富翁，他會向你借錢？

Mary: I'm dead serious.

我是說真的。

The dirt is that Tom's father lost all his money in the stock market.

有謠言說，湯姆父親所有的錢都在股票市場賠光了。

John: Don't give me that bullshit.
別胡說八道。

Tom's father is not green in the stock market.
湯姆的父親又不是股市新手。

How could he lose all his money?
怎麼會把錢全部賠光？

Mary: Beats me.
我怎麼知道。

Chapter 9

Come down on someone hard
責備；責罵；批評

Mary's parents really came down on her for coming home late.

瑪麗的父母因為她很晚回家而責罵她。

句型解說

　　責罵、責怪或批評是常見的事，常見的英文用法也很多，come down on～是其中之一。如果是説狠狠地責罵，或是批評得很厲害，可以用 come down hard on～，或 come down on someone hard。

1. My mother came down on me because I got home late.
   我媽媽因為我很晚回家而罵我。

2. Don't you think you came down too hard on him for breaking a bowl?
   他不過打破一個碗，你這樣罵他不覺得太過分了嗎？

3. The teacher came down hard on the cheaters.
   老師把考試作弊的人痛罵一頓。

4. Yes, they came down hard on him.
   是的，他們狠狠地把他罵了一頓。

5. The critics came down much too hard on the performance.
   評論家對這次演出的批評太過分了。

Rag on someone

責怪;責罵

My mom ragged on me for coming home late last night.

我媽因為我昨晚太晚回家而罵我。

句型解說

　　父母罵孩子,上司罵下屬,老師罵學生,英文有幾個常用的說法。rag on someone 是其中之一。另有一種說法不是罵,而是嘮叨個不停,英文是 chew on。

舉一反三

類似用語: chew out

　　　　　come down on someone

1. My dad keeps ragging on me about my hair style.
我爸對我的髮型罵個不停。

2. My girlfriend ragged on me for an hour because I forget our date.
我的女朋友罵了我一個小時，因為我忘記我們的約會。

3. My mom always rags on me about my taste in music.
我媽總是我對我的音樂品味有意見。

4. My father chewed me out when I took the car without asking.
我老爸一直罵我，在把車子開走前沒有先問他。

5. My mother always chewing on me to read more books.
我媽一直嘮叨我多看些書。

6. Mary chewed me out for letting her cat out of the house.
瑪麗因為我讓貓跑出屋外而罵我。

Chicken out

臨陣退縮

I was going to ask her out, but I chickened out at the last minute.

本來我想約她出去，但在最後一分鐘我卻臨陣退縮了。

句型解說

　　我們常聽人家笑人膽小鬼，英文 chicken。這裡用做動詞，指膽小退縮，臨陣脫逃。後面加介系詞 out。

靈活運用

1. He was going to ask his boss for a

raise but he chickened out.

他本來想向他的老闆要求加薪，但又臨陣退縮了。

2. Please don't chicken out of this now.

請別到現在才臨陣退縮。

3. Mary: You said you wanted to ask Jane as your date for the dance.

你說你要邀珍妮做你的舞伴。

Where is she?

她人呢？

John: I chickened out.

我臨陣退縮了。

Mary: Don't chicken out.

別臨陣脫逃。

You're almost there.

你已經快成功了。

Keep going.

繼續努力。

You'll make it.

你會成功的。

John: Sorry but I just can't.

很抱歉，但我就是做不到。

Grounded
被禁足；被罰不准

John was grounded.
約翰被罰了。

He can't play Nintendo game until he gets straight A's on the next report card.
除非他下次的成績單上每科都在 90 分以上，否則他不能玩任天堂。

句型解說

　　美國的父母不常打罵孩子，但最常見的處罰方式是禁足、不准看電視或玩任天堂遊戲等。所以美國同學之間常可聽到某人 was grounded，或 got grounded。

1. I got grounded for coming home late the other night.

   我因為前晚太遲回家，被禁足了。

2. I failed my math final, and my parents are going to ground me.

   我的數學期末考不及格，我的父母會把我禁足。

3. Mary was grounded.

   瑪麗被禁足了。

   She can't come to dance tonight.

   她今晚不能來跳舞。

美國的節慶：復活節

　　復活節是春天的星期天，而每年的時間都不一定。復活節源於基督徒相信、並慶祝耶穌被釘十字架後的重生。所以對基督徒而言，這是個充滿宗教恩典及家人團聚的日子。復活節的傳統活動 -- 水煮蛋，並彩繪復活蛋，小朋友還可以得到大人送的糖果呢！

Bummer

真倒楣

So you can't go to the dance after all?

所以，你還是不能去參加舞會？

What a bummer!

怎麼那麼倒楣！

句型解說

　　年輕人常愛說「真倒楣，怎麼那麼倒楣」。如果是用在被老師責罵或是被父母禁足等他們自認倒楣的事，他們會自言自語「bummer」。但若用這個字敘述一件他們認為倒楣的事之後，會加一句「What a bummer!」。

1. Mom:　John, turn off the TV.
約翰，把電視關掉。

　　　　You can't watch TV until you
finish your homework.
功課做完之前，你不可以看電視。

　John:　Bummer!
真倒楣。

2. I can't go with you to the movies tonight because I have to babysit my
little sister.
我今晚不能跟你去看電影，因為我要照顧我妹妹。

What a bummer!
真倒楣。

3. I can't go to the dance, because I got
grounded.
我不能去舞會，因為我被禁足了。

What a bummer!
真倒楣。

Let someone down
令人失望

I'm sorry I let you down.
很抱歉，我令你失望。

句型解說

令別人失望，英文有個單字是 disappoint，但大家可以常常聽到 let ～ down 這個用法。

靈活運用

1. Please don't let me down.
   別讓我失望。

   I am depending on you.
   我全靠你了。

2. I don't want to let you down, but I can't support you in the issue.
我不想讓你失望，但在這個問題上，我不能支持你。

3. Mom: It's raining so hard.
雨下得這麼大。

Are you sure you still want to go out?
你確定要出去嗎？

John: I promised to take Mary to a movie.
我答應要帶瑪麗去看電影。

I can't let her down.
我不能令她失望。

4. Mary: John promised to come to my birthday party.
約翰答應來參加我的生日宴會。

But he didn't show up yet.
但他還沒到。

Dad: Don't worry.
別擔心。

He will come.
他會來的。

He won't let you down.
他不會讓妳失望的。

5. John: I failed the entrance examination.
我入學考試失敗了。

I'm sorry that I let you down.
很抱歉，我令妳失望。

Mom: Don't feel too bad.
別太難過。

Study harder, next year you'll make it.
用功點，明年你一定考得取。

比爾・蓋茨教學生做人（4）

第七、你的學校也許已經不再分優等生和劣等生，但生活卻仍在做出類似的區分。某些學校廢除當人制度，只要你想找到正確答案，學校會給你無數次機會。這和現實生活中的任何事，沒有一點相似之處。

第八、生活不分學期，你並沒有寒暑假可以休息，也沒有幾位雇主樂於幫助你發現自我。自己找時間做吧。

79

Up to no good

惹事生非

I haven't seen John for the weekend.

我整個週末都沒看到約翰。

He must be up to no good.

他準是做了什麼壞事。

句型解說

　　有時我們說到某人，說他喜歡惹事生非，沒看到他就知道他又是去惹事生非了。或是看到他的表情，就知道他又是做了什麼壞事，英文說 up to no good。

1. I could tell from the look on John's face that he was up to no good.

   從約翰臉上的表情我就可以看出來，他準又做了什麼壞事。

2. There are four boys outside the store, I don't know what they are doing, but I think they are up to no good.

   有四個男孩在店外面，我不知道他們在做什麼，但我想他們不會幹什麼好事。

3. I don't know where you hung out all night.

   我不知道你們整晚都在那裡混。

   But I know you are up to no good.

   但我知道你們不會幹什麼好事。

   ### 美國的節慶：聖誕節

   聖誕節是美國的重大節日之一，在每年的 12 月 25 日，是慶祝耶穌基督的聖誕。在美國，聖誕節的氣氛很濃厚，家家戶戶都會有聖誕樹，並用溫暖的燈光、絢麗的彩帶、飾品，裝點得十分美麗，每個人都會交換禮物、送卡片，是個很溫馨的節日。

Dweeb

笨蛋，令人討厭的人

You like him?
妳喜歡他？
He's such a dweeb.
他是笨蛋一個。

句型解說

　　年輕人喜歡交朋友，但是有些人卻不受歡迎，同學間喜歡拿他當作取笑的對象。這些取笑的話英語有很多，但依個人的表現，招致取笑的因素不一樣，有不同的英文字來叫他們。

　　下面這幾個字都有白痴、笨蛋、令人討厭的意思：dweeb, geek 和 dork，至於 goof 則含有笨拙的意思。另

外一個英文字 nerd 卻與白痴、笨蛋相反,語氣中除了譏笑還有嫉妒的味道。nerd 是指書呆子,尤其是在數理、科學方面很強,這種人戴著厚厚的眼鏡,卻不會交際應酬,穿著品味更是令人發笑。

靈活運用

1. She is such a geek.
   她實在是個白痴。

2. Mary may have looked like a geek before, but you should see her now.
   瑪麗以前像個白痴,但你應該看看現在的她。

3. Jenny couldn't believe her best friend would go out with such a dork.
   珍妮不敢相信她最好的朋友竟會跟這樣一個笨蛋約會。

4. John felt like a goof after he screwed up his act in the school talent show.
   約翰在學校的才藝表演搞砸之後,他就顯得很笨拙。

5. John wasn't unpopular, but he was considered a bit of a science nerd.
   約翰也不是不受歡迎,只是大家認為他像個科學怪人

Get lost
迷路；走失了；走開

We got lost on the way to Mary's home.
到瑪麗家的路上我們迷路了。

句型解說

　　get lost 大家都知道這句話指迷路的意思。但它還有另一個意思，指別人來煩你，你叫他走開，也可以說 get lost 或 go away。

舉一反三

Stop bugging me.　Get lost!
別煩我，走開！

1. Get lost! I don't need your help.
   走開！我不需要你的幫忙。

2. Stop follwing me. Get lost!
   別跟著我，走開。

3. John: Hi, I'm John.
   嗨！我是約翰。

   Want to dance?
   妳要跳舞嗎？

   Mary: No, thanks.
   不，謝謝。

   John: Aw, come on.
   噢！來吧！

   Mary: I said no thanks.
   我剛剛說了，不，謝謝。

   Now get lost!
   請你馬上離開。

Zit

青春痘

I can't believe I got this huge zit the day before the prom.

我不敢相信在畢業舞會的前一天，我長了這麼大一顆青春痘。

句型解說

青春痘是每位青少年的煩惱，一般的說法是 pimple。但年輕人和學生另有流行的叫法是 zit 或 zun。

靈活運用

Is that a zit I see ruining your pretty face?
我看把妳漂亮的臉蛋破壞的，是不是那顆青春痘？

I'm deeply troubled by the zits on my face.
我被臉上這些青春痘煩死了。

Hang out

瞎混

I wish you wouldn't hang out all night.

我希望你別整晚瞎混。

句型解說

hang out 是指在某地逗留、浪費時間。後面也可以加個地方，指在那個地方逗留、浪費時間。也可以加 with 某人，指與某人在一起瞎混浪費時間。

1. Why do you have to hang out near the place?
   你們為何要在那種地方瞎混呢？

2. You guys spent too much time hanging out.
   你們花太多時間瞎混了。

3. Mary: Is this where you guys hang out all the time?
   這兒就是你們一天到晚鬼混的地方嗎？

   John: Yes, do you like it?
   是啊！妳喜歡嗎？

Hang out with~

跟某人一起瞎混

You hang out with John too much.
你跟約翰一起混太久了。

句型解說

　　hang out 是瞎混，浪費時間的意思。後面加 with 某人，表示跟某人在一起瞎混，浪費時間。

靈活運用

1. I wish you would stop hanging out with those boys.

我希望妳別再跟那些男孩鬼混了。

You are a grown-up now.

妳已經長大了。

2. Don't hang out with those girls.

不要跟那些女孩子一起瞎混。

They are not your type.

她們跟妳不同類。

3. Mary likes to hang out with those boys.

瑪麗喜歡跟那些男孩子一起鬼混。

She thinks they are fun to be with.

她以為那很好玩。

But I know those kids are always looking for trouble.

但我知道他們是專門找麻煩的。

Get on my nerves

惹我厭煩；令我神經緊張

Stop whinning.
別哭！
It's getting on my nerves.
煩死了

句型解說

　　nerve 是神經，get on my nerves 令我很煩、令我神經緊張。另有一個英文字 annoy 也是表示此一說法的常見字。

1. That noise is getting on my nerves.
那個噪音實在令我心煩。

2. She's always late for our dates.
我們的約會她常常遲到。

It's annoying.
實在令人很煩。

3. Please turn the radio down.
請把收音機關小一點。

It's getting on my nerves.
它實在讓我很煩。

4. John: The girl next to me kept talking and talking throughout the class.
坐在我隔壁的女孩子整堂課一直說個不停。

It's getting on my nerves.
煩死了。

Mary: You should've paid attention to the teacher, not the girl.
你應該專心聽老師上課,不是那女孩子。

MP3-87

Clean up one's act

好好表現；改善行為

If you don't clean up your act, you'll get canned.

如果你不好好表現的話，你會被開除。

句型解說

　　clean up one's act 指某人行為或是表現令人不滿意。可用於員工在公司的表現，學生在校的行為或是在家的行為等。

靈活運用

1. Since Mary cleaned up her act,

everyone liked her.

自從瑪麗改善她的行為後，大家都很喜歡她。

2. If you want to join us, you'd better clean up your act.

如果你想加入我們的話，你的行為最好改一改。

3. You can't go to the movies until you clean up your act.

除非你把你的行為改好，否則你不能去看電影。

會話練習

John:	How about going to a movie to-night?
	今晚去看電影好嗎？
Mary:	I'm sorry I can't.
	很抱歉，我不能去
John:	Come on.
	來嘛！
	Don't let me down.
	別讓我失望。
Mary:	But I got grounded.
	但是我被禁足了。
Mary:	Last night I came home too late.
	昨晚我回家太晚了。

My mom came down hard on me.

我媽狠狠罵了我一頓。

Now, until I clean up my act I can't go out in the evening.

在我好好表現一番之前，我晚上是不能出去的。

John: Bummer!

真倒楣！

Mary: Besides, my mom said I hang out with you too much.

還有我媽說我和你在一起瞎混太多了。

I'm afraid I can't go out with you anymore.

我恐怕以後不能再和你出去了。

Chapter

MP3-88

Two thumbs up!

非常好。

His performance in the play
deserved two thumbs up.

他在劇中的表現非常好。

句型解說

　　美國電視上有個非常受歡迎的影評節目。兩位影評人評論電影，只用豎起大姆指或指向地上表示一部電影的好壞。這兩位影評人意見經常不同。看他們兩個人為一部電影的好壞爭論是很有趣的事。

　　有時候，他們對一部電影也有意見一致，同時舉起大姆指的時候，如陳凱歌導演的「霸王別姬」，這就是 Two thumbs up! 所以這句話，也變成美國最流行的用語之一。

類似用語： Great! 太棒了

I like the movie. I think it's great.

我喜歡這部電影。我認為很棒。

Wonderful! 好極了。

Excellent! 太好了。

相反用語： awful 太差了

I can't believe she would dress like a bean bag. She looked awful.

我不敢相信她會穿得像一個大草包。難看極了！

out of character. 離譜

Sharon Stone's performance in Sliver was absolutely out of character. She could be better.

莎朗史東在「銀色獵物」中的表現太離譜了，她應該可以更好。

靈活運用

1. Mary: What do you think of Jurassic Park?

你看「侏羅紀公園」如何？

John: Two thumbs up!

非常好！

2. John: Jenny wears a new hairstyle.

珍妮換了新髮型。

I am not too crazy about it.

我不太喜歡。

What do you think?

你看呢？

Mary: I give her two thumbs up.

我看非常好。

MP3-89

Hold your tongue!

不要再說

Hold your tongue. You have said enough already.

不要再說了。你已經說夠了。

句型解說

　　十七、八歲之所以為稱為人生的黃金時期，是因為有太多的事可成為秘密，可以當作悄悄話來說，要是大聲嚷嚷，路人皆知，那就沒意思了。所以美國年輕人是很在意別人說話的。萬一有人忍不住要將秘密說出來，就趕快警告他 Hold your tongue!

舉一反三

類似用語： Stop! 別說了。

Stop! Don't say anything more.

閉嘴，別再說了。

keep it to yourself. 自己知道就好。

Hey, dude, watch your big mouth.

嗨，朋友。別口沒遮攔的。

You'd better keep it to yourself

自己知道就好了。

相反用語： speak out 說出來

Don't keep it to yourself. Speak out.

別把事情悶在心裡，說出來。

Spit it out. 把話說出來。

Come on. I know you have something to say.

來吧！我知道你有話要說。

Spit it out! 講出來吧！

（靈活運用）

1. Bill: You're seeing Henry a lot, aren't you?

你跟亨利約會很多次，不是嗎？

You are in love, Mary.

瑪麗，妳 愛了！

Mary: Hold your tongue, Bill!

比爾，不要再說了！

2. Mary: Stop! You have said enough.

不要再說了，你說夠了！

Bill: You can't make me hold my tongue.

你不能叫我不說。

I am going to spit everything out.

我要把一切都講出來。

Take a nose dive.

直線下墜

Mary's grades took a nose dive.
瑪麗的成績直線下墜。

句型解說

　　年輕人說話要趕流行，不然就太遜了。帶有圖畫效果的話，總是最容易流行。像「下降」、「退步」這類的話，若是用 drop 或 drop a lot 就太不夠性格了。你看過飛機掉下來吧！機翼朝下，直線式的下墜才能達到「話中有畫」的戲劇效果。

　　Take a nose dive 理所當然的成為流行美語之一。

相似用語：go down 下墜

Sharon Stone's movies may not have good box office, but her popularity does not go down a bit.

莎朗史東的電影票房也許不好，但她受歡迎程度一點都沒有下降。

相反用語：rocket 衝上天

The car price is rocketing.

汽車價格暴漲。

靈活運用

1. Mary: I am kind of worrying about my Dad.

   我有些擔心我老爹。

   His health took a nose dive in the last couple of months.

   這幾個月以來，他的健康狀況直線下降。

   John: Come on. Loosen up. He'll be all right.

   好了，放輕鬆點，他沒問題的。

2. Mary: How come your math grades took a nose dive?

   你的數學成績為什麼直線下降？

   John: Beats me. I tried as hard as I did before.

   天曉得。我跟以前一樣用功。

No-show

爽約；不來

I don't see Mary.
It looks like she is a no-show.
我沒看見瑪麗。她似乎爽約了。

句型解說

　　美國年輕人最喜歡運動。大學校園和高中校園中的英雄必然是美式足球球員。每次比賽，必然是全校總動員，雖然票價很貴，但還是場場客滿。隔天的報紙不但報導戰況，還要報導總共賣出多少票，多少人進場，多少人買了票臨時沒出席。

　　這些沒出席的叫 no-show。美國年輕人把跟人家約好卻臨時爽約的，也叫做 no-show 。

相似用語： not coming. 不來了

Where is Mary? 瑪麗在那裡？

Is she not coming? 她不來了嗎？

相反用語： show up 出席

Turn up. 出席

Mary turned up in the party.

瑪麗在派對中露面。

1. Mary: Jenny told me she would come to the party, but so far I haven't seen her show up yet.
   珍妮告訴我她會來參加派對，但直到現在我還沒見到她。

   John: Jenny always promises too easily. So, don't be surprised if she turned out to be a no-show.
   珍妮常常很輕易答應人家。所以要是她爽約不來，別太訝異。

2. Mary: Loosen up. You look pretty harsh.
   放輕鬆點。你看起來很兇！

   John: I am pissed off. Jenny was supposed to meet me at the movie theater. We were going to see the movie, but she truned out to be a no-show.
   我氣瘋了！珍妮原該在戲院前跟我碰面。我們約好一起看電影的，結果她竟然沒來！

Put up with something
忍受

I can't put up with the noise any longer.
我不能再忍受這種噪音。

句型解說

　　這不是一句新的用語，但卻是流行不衰。學校裡考單字時老師喜歡用難字出題，往往叫學生背 tolerate 或 tolerance，實際上用 tolerate 表示忍受，帶有姑息的意思，用在否定句。

　　像上面一句例句，指噪音用 tolerate 完全不合適。而 put up with 用起來就有彈性多了。指人、事、物都可以用，而且字又簡單，還是將這個語句記熟，多用吧！

相似用語：take it 忍受

a. Her comment about me is getting out of hand.

她說我的閒話越來越離譜。

b. I am not going to take it any longer.

我不能再忍受了！

Stick it out. 再撐一下！

The pain will soon be over. Stick it out.

痛一下就過去了，再撐一會兒。

相反用語：Out of patience 沒有耐心

The game was so boring that the audience were all out of patience after awhile.

比賽很沈悶。觀眾一下子就沒有耐心看下去。

1. Mary: Mr. Lin treats his wife like dirt.

林先生把他太太當作一文不值。

I wonder how she could put up with him for so long.

我真不明白她怎麼能忍耐這麼久。

John: Mind your own business.

管好妳自己！

Keep your nose out of it.

不要管閒事。

2. John: What's that smell?
什麼味道？

Would you please open the window, Mary?
瑪麗，請打開窗子好嗎。

I can't put up with the smell anymore.
我受不了這種味道。

Mary: All right, I will open the window.
好，我來開窗。

I can't take the smell, either.
我也受不了這種味道。

Bean brain

蠢材，沒腦筋

John is such a bean brain. He can never understand what's going on.

約翰是個蠢材。他老是搞不清狀況。

句型解說

　　流行英語裡大部分是罵人的，像這個 bean brain 就是説別人腦筋只有一顆豆子大，笨得要命。美國年輕人，尤其是校園中，常互相嘲笑對方是 bean brain，有時已經變成一種好玩的説法。bean 又可以與 know 連用，但只用在否定句，表示一點概念都沒有，請看下面的例句：

I don't know beans about cars.

我對汽車一竅不通。

類似用語：airhead 腦袋空空

John proved to be an airhead when he suggested we all cheat on the exam.

約翰建議我們大家一起作弊，這證明他沒腦筋。

相反用語：sharp 反應敏捷

Bill is very sharp.

比爾反應很靈敏。

smart 聰明

Mary is very smart in math.

瑪麗數學很行。

clever 精明

中學教科書中說 clever 是聰明的意思。在某些場合中，這個解釋是可以的。但說話中 clever 不要隨便用，因為 clever 指一個人很精明，有時候帶有嘲諷的意思。請看下面的例子。

John is clever.　He won't be fooled.

約翰精明得很，不會受騙的。

John:　I can't imagine Bill is such a bean brain.

無法想像比爾怎麼這麼沒腦筋。

Mary:　Why do you say that?

你為什麼那樣說？

John:　He was supposed to take a picture of all of our class.

他想為全班同學照像。

He brought the camera and forgot the film.

他相機帶了，卻忘了帶底片。

93

Big-mouth

口沒遮攔，大嘴巴

Bill has a big-mouth.
He cannot keep secret.
比爾是個大嘴巴，不能保守秘密。

句型解說

　　在所有流行美語中最容易使用又不會用錯的，就是這個 big-mouth。它可以用在句子裡，也可以單獨使用來罵人愛說話。任何人說話不看場合，或是不該說的話卻一直說，都可以用 Big-mouth 來「尊稱」他。對有 big mouth 的人，不提防一些是不行的。

相似用語：gossiper 三姑六婆

Don't tell Mary anything. She is a big gossiper.

別告訴瑪麗任何事，她會像三姑六婆一樣到處廣播。

相反用語：clam up 像蛤一樣閉得緊緊的。

When I asked him if he saw who stole my purse, he clammed up.

當我問他是否看見誰偷我錢包，他閉嘴不說。

1. Shut up your big mouth!

閉上你的大嘴巴。

2. Be careful when you talk to Mary. She has a big mouth.

跟瑪麗說話要小心，她是個大嘴巴。

3. It takes actions to get things done, not just a big mouth.

事情要成功需靠行　，不只是嘴巴說說。

4. No one can put up with Mary's big mouth.

沒有人能忍受瑪麗的大嘴巴。

94

Red-hot

紅得發紫，搶手

The Dallas Cowboys are red-hot.
They won two Superbowls in a row.
達拉斯牛仔隊正紅得發紫，他們連續贏得兩屆超級杯。

句型解說

又紅又熱表示很搶手，可別誤以為是很燙手噢！凡是受歡迎的東西和人物都可以用 red-hot 來形容。

舉一反三

相似用語：very cool 很拉風

The motorcycle is very cool. A lot of

people want to buy it.

這款摩托車很拉風。好多人想買。

相反用語：hot potato 燙手山芋；沒人要

The traffic issue in Taipei is a hot potato.

台北市交通問題沒人敢碰。

靈活運用

1. Mary:　The pro baseball in Taiwan is red-hot.

台灣職棒很熱門。

John:　Yes, you can hardly get a ticket if you don't reserve early.

是啊！不預先買票就一票難求。

2. Computer science is red-hot in college.

大學電腦系很熱門。

3. The 1995 TOYOTA Corolla is red-hot in the market.

一九九五年豐田可樂娜車型在市場上大受歡迎。

Hardcore!

很難的課程，硬漢

I passed all the hardcores this semester.

我這學期所有難修的課程都過關了。

句型解說

　　core 是果核，咬它的時候要小心，弄不好，它硬得把你的門牙都扳歪了。美國流行口語把 hardcore 拿來形容很難纏的事或人。在年輕人之間，看到很酷的行為，也可以用 Hardcore! 來表示支持或欣賞；校園中則拿 hardcores 來指很困難的課程，通常用複數形式比較多。

　　總之 hardcore 是很年輕的流行美語。上班族用起來，也使人覺得特別精神。講 Hardcore! 表示「哇！好傢伙，

夠勇敢！」的時候，把左手舉起來，互相在空中對拍一下，
give me five! 更傳神。

相似用語：Tough! 夠生猛；夠難纏

Bill is very tough. Do not mess with
him.

比爾很難纏，別招惹他。

Math is a tough subject. It requires a
lot of work to be good at it.

數學是很難纏的科目，須要下很大功夫才能學
好。

Life is tough!

人生不如意之事十常八九。

相反用語：A piece of cake. 手到擒來

Math is a piece of cake to me. I can
always ace it easily.

數學對我來說太簡單了，我隨時都可以輕鬆地
拿到滿分。

1. Mary: Bill is very tough and people try
to shun him.

比爾很難纏，大家都儘量躲開他。

But John called him a jerk to
his face today.

而約翰今天當著他的面叫他渾球。

That pissed Bill off real bad.
那使比爾很感冒。

David: Wow, hardcore! Go, John, go!
哇！太帥了！加油，約翰加油。

2. John: I wonder why school life has to be so tough.
我不懂學校生活為什麼這麼難。

Mary: Why do you say that?
你為什麼這麼說？

John: Well, you have all these harecores to take.
喏，你得讀那麼多困難的課程。

Mary: Oh, give me a break. You are smart. You can handle them.
得了吧！你那麼聰明，可以應付自如啦！

Out of the blue

毫無來由;不知從哪裡冒出來

Out of the blue

I bombed on my test today.
我今天考砸了!
All the questions were out of the blue.
所有的題目都不知從哪那裡冒出來的。

句型解說

　　美國口語實在很可愛。尤其流行口語更是「話中有畫」,像這句 out of the blue,就像在茫茫大海,蒼天一色的情況下,突然冒出個東西來,不知是出自蔚藍的海,還是降自蔚藍的天,令人兩眼一愣。這句話也可以說成 out of the clear blue,指光天化日之下,不知哪裡冒出

來的東西。

相似用語：out of nowhere　突然冒出來
The other car appeared out of nowhere.
另一部車不知從哪裡突然冒出來。
without cause　沒有理由
Your accusation of my stealing is without cause.
你指控我偷竊是沒有理由的。

靈活運用

1. I received a letter out of the blue. In it someone said I owed him money.
我突然收到一封來路不明的信。寫信的人說我欠他錢。

2. My science teacher is weird. He always asks the questions out of the blue.
我的自然老師很奇怪，老喜歡問一些稀奇古怪的問題。

3. My accusation is not out of the blue. I have proof.
我的指控不是憑空捏造的，我有證據。

CHAPTER 10

Scream
熱鬧；有意思

The movie was a scream.
這部電影很有意思，很好看。

句型解說

　　越是流行的口語越是簡單。困難的字誰還會去用？像這個 scream 原意是「尖叫」，美國年輕人拿來指一切可以讓你興奮得尖叫的東西。電影是一個好例子，帥哥也是另一個好例子。

舉一反三

相似用語：hilarious 熱鬧令人興奮

His performance in the play is hilarious.

他在劇中的表現很好。

相反用語：sleeper 沈悶得讓人睡著

Don't go to the movie. It's a sleeper.

不要去看那部電影，它沈悶得叫你睡著。

靈活運用

1. Modonna's concert is a scream. You've got to see it.

瑪丹娜的演唱會很熱鬧，你必須去瞧一瞧。

2. The whole show was a scream. The audience were so excited that you could feel the stadium trembling.

整場表演好熱鬧。觀眾興奮得讓你可以感到整個體育館都在震 。

Corny

陳腔濫調

The dress is corny.
這套衣服式樣又老又俗氣。

句型解說

　　Corny 這個字原本聲勢不高，因為美國冬季奧運溜冰銀牌得主南茜凱莉根了迪斯耐公司兩百萬美金，跟米老鼠及唐老鴨同坐一部花車，原本應該是一場廣告秀，南茜卻一路嘮叨，嫌兩隻卡通人物太 corny，不料被麥克風傳了出來，讓所有人一陣錯愕。也因為南茜的沒有風度，使 corny 這個字再度風行。

　　美國家庭中，多少父母為了兒女的樣樣嫌 corny 而傷腦筋。美國影評家乾脆畫一支玉米 corn 來表示一部電影的陳腔濫調。要是以排行榜來看，corny 應是老歌新唱，高居前幾名。

相似用語：fossil 化石；老掉牙

Bill is a fossil in my class. I don't know when he will graduate.

在我們班上，比爾是個老化石，留級好多次，不知道幾時才能畢業。

old school 老派

It is old school thinking that women should stay at home.

女人應該乖乖在家是老式思想。

相反用法：catch one's eye 亮麗耀眼

The bule jacket really caught my eye.

藍色夾克真是亮麗耀眼。

靈活運用

1. Bill: How was the movie?
   電影好看嗎？

   Mary: It was corny, a waste of my money.
   陳腔濫調, 浪費我的錢。

2. Bill: Stop reading those romance fictions.
   不要再讀那些羅曼史小說了。

   All they have are nothing but corny love stories.
   他們寫的無非是老掉牙的愛情故事。

   Mary: If there is anything corny, that is your thinking toward romance.
   要是有誰老掉牙，那就是你對羅曼史的觀念。

Uh, Oh!

唉呀！糟糕！

Uh, oh!   I locked   my   key   in   my car.

唉呀，糟糕，我把車輪匙鎖在車裡了！

句型解說

　　要測驗會不會說美語，就看那個人遇到緊急情況時會不會很自然地用美式反應。像"Ouch!"，"Oh, No!"這種哼哼哈哈的短句，不學還真的不會。要是與美國朋友同行，他突然叫聲"Uh, Oh!"，你還不知道趕快表示關切地回答"What's wrong?"或"Something wrong?"，那你就夠失禮了。這種短句語調很重要，務必要聽 MP3，跟著學習。

相似用語：Oh, No! 唉呀，完了！

Oh, no! The rain is coming down. I left the windows open at home.

唉呀，完了！下雨了，我家裡窗戶沒有關。

Oh, man! 唉呀，怎麼搞的！

Oh, man! Look what you have done to my car.

唉呀，怎麼搞的。看你把我車子弄得這樣！

相反用語：Oh, yes! 太好了

Oh, yes! The typhoon is coming. There will be no school tomorrow.

太好了！颱風來了！明天不上課！

靈活運用

1. Uh, oh! Here he comes!
   唉呀，糟糕，他來了！〈不想見他〉

2. Uh, oh! I forgot to bring money.
   唉呀，糟糕，我忘了帶錢。

3. Uh, oh! I left my purse in the restroom.
   唉呀！糟糕！我把錢包留在洗手間。

4. Mary: Uh, oh!
   唉呀，糟糕！

   Bill: Something wrong?
   出什麼錯了？

   Mary: I brought the wrong textbook.
   我帶錯課本了！

Brother!

唉呀！幫個忙！拜託！

Oh, brother! I can't believe you could lose the money.

拜託！我不敢相信你竟然把錢弄丟了！

句型解說

　　Brother！不是叫哥哥，幫個忙也不是真正請人幫忙，而是表示「拜託，你怎麼會這樣」的意思。這句話充滿挫折感，只差沒開口罵人。在語氣上，brother 和 oh 要連著講，不要分開。注意聽 MP3 上的說法，照著學就行。

舉一反三

相似用語：Come on! 怎麼可能！〈on 的尾音稍拉長。〉

Come on! Don't tell me you lost the money.

唉呀，怎麼可能！別跟我説你把錢弄丟了！

Oh, no! 唉呀；糟糕

Oh, no! Did you really lose the money?

唉呀，糟糕，你真的把錢丟了？

Oh, my! 唉呀，真要命！

Oh, my! How could you lose the money?

唉呀，真要命，你怎麼可以把錢弄丟呢？

靈活運用

1. Oh, brother!　See how much homework we have today.

   唉呀，幫幫忙！今天功課好多。

2. Oh, brother!　Next time, would you please be on time？

   唉呀，拜託。下次請準時一點好嗎？

3. Oh, brother!　Give me a break.

   唉呀，幫個忙。算了吧！

4. Oh, brother!　The test was so hard.

   唉呀，幫個忙。考試好難噢！

會話練習

John:　　Hey, look who's here?

　　　　嗨！看誰在這裡啊？

Mary:	Oh, hello, John.　Are you coming for the movie? 噢！哈囉，比爾。你來看電影嗎？
John:	No, I just came out of it. 不，我剛看完出來。
Mary:	Which one? 那一部？
John:	Sleepless In Seattle. 「西雅圖夜未眠」。
Mary:	I heard it was very corny. 我聽說它的情節很老套。
John:	No, not at all.　It was hilarious. I gave it two thumbs up. 不，它很有意思。我給它評價很好！
	Do you want me to tell you the story? 要不要我告訴妳它的故事？
Mary:	No, thanks.　Keep it to yourself. I may see it later. 不，謝謝，我也許會去看。
John:	I hope you don't think I am a big mouth. 但願妳不會嫌我多嘴。
	Are you coming alone? 妳自己一個人來嗎？

Mary:	No, Mike was supposed to meet me here, but it has passed the show time. 不，邁可應該在這裡與我碰面，但開演時間都過了。
John:	Uh, Oh! Don't tell me he was a no-show. 唉呀！別告訴我他爽約了！
Mary:	He had better shows up soon. Or I will beat up his bean brain. 哼！他最好快點來，不然我打破他的豬頭！
John:	(Loudly)Wow, hardcore! Don't put up with it. Do it, Mary! 〈大聲地〉哇！帥啊！不要姑息他，瑪麗，打破他的腦袋！
Mary:	Hold your tongue, please. 小聲一點。
John:	I was just joking. Well, see you later. I hope Mike will appear out of the blue to save his own bean brain. 我只是開玩笑。好了，再見。我希望邁可會突然冒出來，以挽救他的腦袋。
Mary:	Oh, brother. Get going! See you later. 唉！幫個忙！快走吧！再見。

流行美語排行榜-美國人最愛說的100句話

英語系列：49

作者／張瑪麗
出版者／哈福企業有限公司
地址／新北市板橋區五權街16號
電話／(02) 2945-6285　傳真／(02) 2945-6986
郵政劃撥／31598840　戶名／哈福企業有限公司
出版日期／2018年6月
定價／NT$ 299元 (附MP3)

全球華文國際市場總代理／采舍國際有限公司
地址／新北市中和區中山路2段366巷10號3樓
電話／(02) 8245-8786　傳真／(02) 8245-8718
網址／www.silkbook.com 新絲路華文網

香港澳門總經銷／和平圖書有限公司
地址／香港柴灣嘉業街12號百樂門大廈17樓
電話／(852) 2804-6687　傳真／(852) 2804-6409
定價／港幣100元 (附MP3)

email／haanet68@Gmail.com
網址／Haa-net.com
facebook／Haa-net 哈福網路商城

國家圖書館出版品預行編目資料

流行美語排行榜-美國人最愛說的100句
話　/ 張瑪麗著. -- 新北市：哈福企業,
2018.06
　面；　公分. --（英語系列；49）
ISBN 978-986-96282-1-1(平裝附光碟片)
1.英語 2.會話

805.188　　　　　　　　107007750

哈福